FOR TODAY'S CUB SCOUT

SBN 361 02017 1
Copyright ©, 1972, PURNELL & SONS, LTD.
Made and printed in Great Britain by
Purnell & Sons Ltd.,
Paulton (Somerset) and London

THE SIXER ANNUAL 1973

for all Cub Scouts

Illustrated by JERRY MALONE

PURNELL
London, W.1

Andrew and Robert try a "flight" in a Short Sherpa, a research plane given the name "Sherpa" soon after the conquest of Everest by Sir Edmund Hilary and Sherpa Tensing the day before H.M. the Queen was crowned. This plane was the only one of its kind built

Geoffrey joins Robert in a Miles Magister, a little wooden plane in which, with the Tiger Moth biplane, nearly all wartime R.A.F. pilots learned to fly. Its 130-h.p. De Havilland Gypsy Major engine gave it a maximum speed of 145 m.p.h.

THEY FLEW FOR FREEDOM

Cub Scouts in the Pilots' Seats of Famous Aircraft of World War II

by the Editor

Photos by Harry Hammond

Museums are often pretty stuffy places, but not so the Skyfame Aircraft Museum at Staverton Airport, near Gloucester and Cheltenham. It is a thrilling place. I had to pull the three Cub Scouts who came with me out of the pilots' seats or they'd be there still, releasing imaginary bombs or taking evasive action from attacking enemy planes or carrying vital supplies in a transport plane through heavy flak.

The Cub Scouts were Robert Newbery, Geoffrey Isaac and Andrew Hoblin, of the 1st Hatherley Pack, and they spent the day looking over aircraft that were keeping the skyways of the world free before they were born—in World War II, 1939-1945.

One of the most fascinating things about the Skyfame Aircraft Museum is that you can see all the planes at close quarters. The Cubs climbed into most of them, operated the controls,

It's a thrill for Geoffrey and Robert to be at the controls of a huge four-engined Handley Page Hastings transport plane. This, the largest plane with the R.A.F. when it entered service in 1947, could carry loads of up to ten tons and did great service airlifting supplies to Berlin when all road and rail routes to the West were cut off for more than a year

All young visitors to the Skyfame Museum delight in the Percival Proctor. They go right into the cockpit, handle the controls, and "learn to fly on the ground". Geoffrey and Robert (in the photograph) and Andrew would have stayed there all day! The Percival Proctor was powered by a De Havilland Gypsy Queen engine of 210-h.p. and could reach a speed of 195 m.p.h.

The three Cubs are inspecting the Airspeed Oxford advanced trainer designed by the famous author Neville Shute. The Duke of Edinburgh won his R.A.F. wings on this type, as did over 8,000 Commonwealth pilots. Two 375-h.p. Armstrong Siddeley Cheetah engines give it a top speed of 182 m.p.h. This plane is the only one of three left in Britain that can still fly

The three Cubs smile as they stand on the wing of a Hawker Tempest, and well they might, for this superb fighter destroyed twenty fast German jet fighters and by far the greatest number of pilotless flying bombs, which, alone of all defending fighters, it could easily catch. It was powered by 2,000-h.p. Bristol Centaurus engines, and could fly at 500 m.p.h.

and did practically everything but fly.

Most of the aircraft here are priceless. One or two are the only survivors of their type left in the world, and every one of them are genuine, battle-scarred veterans that operated in the heat and fury of a war the like of which we all pray may never again devastate the world. In the sunshine and warmth of a sunny day it wasn't easy for the Cubs to realise the terrible conditions—the hostility, the danger, the

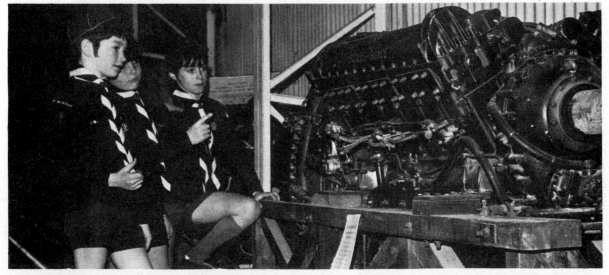

Geoffrey, Andrew and Robert look with awe on the most successful aero engine ever designed, the Rolls Royce Merlin, which developed first 1,000 h.p. and finally 1,800 h.p. More than 150,000 of these engines were fitted to Hurricanes, Spitfires, Mosquitoes, Lancasters, Halifaxes, Defiants, Fulmars, Whitleys and Battles, as well as to American Mustangs, Kitty Hawks and Argonauts

Guess what machine lies behind the propeller the Cubs are trying to swing. It's an Avro Cierva 30 Autogiro, designed by Juan de la Cierva and fitted with a 150-h.p. Armstrong Siddeley Genet Major engine. The autogiro could take off and land vertically, but was not able to stand still in the air like the helicopter that succeeded it

mention in detail. The photograph in colour on the cover of this annual shows Robert, Geoffrey and Andrew with some of the models.

Mr Peter Thomas, who is the founder of the Skyfame Aircraft Museum, welcomes parties of visitors, as well as individuals, so if your Pack is near enough to Staverton to pay a visit it would make a most thrilling objective for a Pack outing. It is open every day, including Sundays, and special rates are in operation for parties. **—R.M.**

second-by-second suspense—endured by the men who flew these machines of war thirty years ago, but the aircraft bear the marks and signs of what they went through.

The aircraft include a helicopter, a biplane trainer, a Mosquito—the "wooden wonder" of World War II—an autogiro, a flying-boat, a bomber, and various naval planes. See if you can spot the type of plane in each photograph before you read the caption.

A room in the museum that the Cubs found very interesting contains a really wonderful collection of model aircraft. There are too many there to

There is a fascinating collection of model aircraft at the Skyfame Museum. One section shows British military flying from before World War I to the jump-jet of today. Another shows the history of flight from the Wright biplane to the space capsule. The Cubs were allowed to take models outside (see top left-hand photograph on next page and front cover of this annual)

The Cubs were joined by two Scouts from the 1st Hatherley Group as they mounted steps (right-hand photograph) to explore the four-engined Handley Page Hastings transport plane, the controls of which they are handling in the photograph on page 7. The Hastings was powered by four 1,650-h.p. Bristol Hercules engines, and with a maximum speed of 354 m.p.h. was very fast for transport aircraft of the 1940's and 1950's. It was much used for training parachute troops, many of which have visited the one in this photograph, TG 528, in which they trained

Now they've got themselves into another plane! This time it's into a Chilton D.W.1.A, which won the King's Air Race once after World War II ended. Five of these little racers were built, and there are two still flying. Power came from a 60-h.p. engine, which gave the plane a very fast speed for its day

STRANGE FLIGHT

by PHILIP J. RANDALL

The monk raised his hand in greeting

"Don't get too wrapped up in that model, Kevin. You mustn't be late for Pack Meeting on your very first night as a Sixer, you know."

"I thought I'd do a bit to this before I went, Mum," Kevin answered.

"This" was a model aircraft Kevin was building as part of his Gold Arrow tests.

As he worked, Kevin thought how small his model would have looked beside the actual aircraft. "I wonder what the first aeroplane men would think if they could come back! Let's see, who was the first Englishman to fly?" Kevin squeezed a spot of clear adhesive on to the end of a sharpened matchstick. "Shall have to work fast. This stuff dries very quickly."

Then he was no longer standing at the kitchen table. He was treading a footpath through a great meadow. The path led to a heavy wooden bridge over a river. Beyond the river was a cluster of buildings.

Long before he reached the bridge he noticed a figure sitting there—a strange figure—a bald-headed man wearing a very long, light-coloured overcoat.

The man stood up as Kevin set foot on the bridge. Now the Cub saw that he was not such an old man, after all. Nor was he completely bald. Except for a bare patch on top of his head, he had plenty of hair. The long overcoat was actually a robe tied about the middle with a knotted cord.

There were mud-walled houses, and boys in smocks were playing in an open turfed space

"The Lord be with you, my son," said the monk, raising his hand in greeting. His accent was very strange.

Kevin, being a choir-boy as well as a Cub Scout, knew the correct reply.

"And with thy spirit," he remembered to answer.

The monk, too, seemed to have trouble with Kevin's speech, but appeared to be satisfied with the response. He smiled and fell into step as they crossed the bridge.

"I am Brother Oliver. How are you named?" he inquired. He spoke slowly, as if trying to make himself understood by a foreigner.

"They call me Kevin," the Cub replied, also speaking as distinctly as he could.

"Ah, Kevin! No doubt named after the holy Saint Kevin, sometime Abbot of the House in the Valley of the Two Lakes; but you are not Irish, surely?"

Kevin was not at all sure about the first bit, but shook his head in answer to the question.

"Have you journeyed far?" was the monk's next question.

"What do I say to that?" Kevin thought.

"If I don't know where I am, how can I say how far I have come?"

"A fair distance," he answered, just to be on the safe side.

"So it seemed to me," Brother Oliver agreed. "Your dress speaks of outlandish places. Those holy relics on your jerkin tell me that you are a pilgrim."

"Holy relics!", thought Kevin, glancing down at the badges on his jersey. "Wait until I tell Akela that one!" He kept the notion to himself and indicated the buildings, which were now much nearer. "What place is that?" he asked.

Brother Oliver regarded him with mild astonishment. "Why, the Abbey of Malmesbury, of course!"

"Malmesbury," thought Kevin. "I *am* a long way from home."

By this time the river was some distance behind. Brother Oliver and Kevin were much nearer the Abbey. A few rough, mud-walled, straw-thatched houses were grouped about an open space of coarse grass. Some boys were playing on the turf. The boys were about Kevin's age, but were dressed very differently. They wore knee-long smocks of rough material over shapeless trousers. One of them was probably the owner of the small dog which was barking excitedly as it chased some swallows. The birds were swooping low, skimming the grass and, at times, even the dog's nose.

"Marvellous birds!" Kevin remarked.

Brother Oliver shot him a swift look. "Indeed they are," he agreed. He hesitated and then continued, "Some day, men will be able to fly and dive like they do—as free in the air as they are on land and can be in water."

"I am sure they will," Kevin assented.

"Do you really think so?"

"Why—er—yes," Kevin replied, a little disturbed by the intense look in the monk's eyes.

The look passed. "Ah, a fellow prophet! Come with me!" Brother Oliver strode towards the Abbey gatehouse.

The porter greeted the monk respectfully. If he noticed Kevin at all he made no sign. Coming out of the shadow of the gatehouse, monk and Cub Scout stood in a large, sunlit courtyard.

"Which is the tallest building of all these?" Brother Oliver asked.

"That one," replied Kevin, without hesitation, pointing at the one immediately in front of them.

"Exactly! That is the Abbey Church and that is where we are going. Follow me!" Ignoring the great main door of the church, Brother Oliver led the way round to the south porch.

"Reckon I have landed myself somewhere in the eleventh century," Kevin thought as they passed into the church.

Silently, almost stealthily, Brother Oliver pushed open a small door in the wall. Together, they began to mount spiral stone steps. Somewhere high above a

Horrified, Kevin peered over the stonework

heavy bell tolled out resonantly.

Kevin was quite leg-weary when they emerged into the open air at the top of the tower. From that height he could see all the monastery buildings at the same time. The boys still playing on the village green seemed to have bodies but no legs.

"It's all a very long way down," was Kevin's unspoken comment.

His examination of the scene below was cut short when Brother Oliver placed a hand on his shoulder. The monk indicated something lying along one side between the roof and the low parapet. Curiosity aroused, Kevin stepped over to examine the objects. He found them to be contraptions constructed of willow wands and parchment, covered for the most part with goose feathers.

Kevin looked up inquiringly.

"My wings," Brother Oliver explained proudly.

"Your—er—wings?" Kevin queried.

"Yes, mine. I made them. Since you, like me, believe that one day men will fly, yours shall be the privilege of watching my first flight."

"But you can't—not like that! You need ——" Kevin began to protest. Then he stopped. He would never convince this crazy monk that before men could fly—many centuries hence—they would have to wait for the invention of the aeroplane engine.

Fascinated, he watched Brother Oliver strap the long, vaguely bird-shaped wings to his arms. There were small ones for the feet.

Satisfied that all were secure, the monk clambered clumsily on to the parapet. He stood swaying slightly for a few seconds and then extended his arms.

"Don't do it! You'll hurt yourself," Kevin cried, "you can't fly. You'll fall!"

The next moment he was alone on the tower. Horrified, he peeped over the stonework. The monk was madly flapping his wings as he fell—down—down.

"Don't flap—glide! Spread your wings!" Kevin shouted.

Brother Oliver could not possibly have heard, but at that exact second he did hold his arms out, stiffly extended. An air current got under those crude wings and bore him up. He glided forward for a few yards. Then he flapped his wings madly and fell down . . . down.

So, alternately flapping and falling,

The monk, madly flapping his wings, fell down . . . down

"You'll be late for Pack meeting," said his mother, putting her head through the doorway

keeping still and gliding, Brother Oliver proceeded on a descending diagonal from the top of the tower to the ground. Missing the top of the gatehouse by inches, he flapped wildly. The action merely hastened the inevitable crash onto the green, where the boys were standing spellbound watching the approaching object.

The first Englishman to fly landed in a crumpled heap. His flight path, afterwards checked over the ground, measured a little over two hundred yards.

The instant Brother Oliver hit the ground Kevin dashed to the door in the tower roof. As swiftly as safety allowed, he descended the spiral steps. By the time he reached the green, the would-be birdman was surrounded by monks, boys and other villagers. To Kevin's relief, Brother Oliver was sitting up among the debris, groaning. He heard someone say that the monk had broken both legs.

Nobody took any notice of the Cub Scout as he attempted to reach the injured monk. It was as if he had not been there.

Trying to push through the unyielding crowd, Kevin slipped. He put out an arm to save himself and his hand touched something lying on the ground. When he recovered his balance, he looked at the object in his hand—a feather from one of Brother Oliver's ineffective wings. The quill end of the feather still retained a stone-hard blob of glue. That dark-brown substance seemed to hold a strange fascination for Kevin. He felt compelled to fasten his eyes on it, until he could see and think of nothing else. It appeared to grow bigger and bigger—and then, smaller and smaller. Eventually it became a spot of clear adhesive on the end of a sharpened matchstick. The glue was as moist as if it had just been squeezed out of the tube.

He heard his mother's voice. "Now then, Kevin, you'll be late for Pack meeting. I knew you would get absorbed if you started on that model. You look very far away!"

Kevin looked up at her with a smile. She did not know *how* far away he *had* been in such a short time!

COLLECT SHELLS AND SEAWEED

for the Bronze Arrow (Simple Collection)
or the Silver Arrow (Collection)
or the Naturalist badge

If you live by the sea or go for a long enough holiday there you could collect shells and seaweed for the Bronze and Silver Arrow Collections or as part of your studies for the Naturalist badge.

Look for shells at low tide and among rocky pools. If the shells are empty you need only wash them in fresh water, but if anything is inside put them into boiling water. Perhaps Mum will help you with this part. The shells must always be clean and empty. You can sometimes polish them with an old toothbrush.

You will need a tray for your collection. You can easily make one yourself by glueing a number of matchbox trays together, as shown in the picture on the next page. Put a little cotton-wool at the bottom of each tray, and on this place a shell.

You could write the name of each shell neatly and paste it on the front or side of the tray. Some of the shells you might find are drawn on the next

page. They include Heart, Cockle, Razor, Piddock, Scallop, and Mussel, but there are many more kinds.

Seaweed is well worth collecting,

time. This softens the seaweed and also washes the salt out of it.

Now lay the specimen on a piece of clean white paper, taking care to arrange it attractively. Ask Mum to let you have some pieces of muslin or pieces of old sheets. Put several sheets of newspaper on the table. Over these put your first piece of muslin. Lay the paper with seaweed on top of it. Right over this lay a piece of muslin, and then place several folded newspapers over it. On top of all this, place the largest and heaviest books you can find to press the seaweed. Keep it pressed for several days, changing the damp newspapers if necessary, but do not disturb the muslin.

At last you can take off the muslin. Very often the seaweed will be stuck to the paper, quite flat; if not, a little gum will fix it.

for there are many different kinds. It is best to collect the thick varieties, like Bladder-Wrack, which is very common. The very delicate kinds are not easy to handle or keep.

If you bring seaweed home from the seaside it will be dry and hard before you are ready to mount it, so you must place it in hot water for a

Packing Parcels

by Eileen Chivers

Learn to do a packer's knot.
The illustration shows you how

At the jolly Christmas season
It makes me sad to say
That faulty packing is the reason
Many parcels go astray.

Wrap your gifts in pretty paper,
Write a list of contents down,
Put them all together neatly,
Parcel them in paper brown.

Address it well in big bold letters,
Tie each knot both strong and tight,
Write the sender in the corner,
Everything will be all right.

O, LITTLE TOWN OF BETHLEHEM

by PHILLIPS BROOKS

O, little town of Bethlehem,
How still we see thee lie;
Above thy deep and dreamless sleep
The silent stars go by;
Yet in thy dark streets shineth
The everlasting Light;
The hopes and fears of all the years,
Are met in thee tonight.

O, morning stars, together
Proclaim the holy birth,
And praises sing to God the King,
And peace to men on earth;
Where charity stands watching
And faith holds wide the door,
The dark night wakes, the glory breaks
And Christmas comes once more.

How silently, how silently,
The wondrous gift is given;
So God imparts to human hearts
The blessings of His heaven.
No ear may hear his coming,
But in this world of sin,
Where meekness will receive him, still
The dear Christ enters in.

ROPE TRICKS

by ALAN WARD

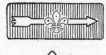

A VANISHING KNOT

"It's fun to tie a knot that's not!" As you say this, you tie a large thumb-knot in a length of soft white rope (or a pyjama cord). Then you blow on the knot, and it simply falls apart! The effect is startling, and audiences love it.

To tie the vanishing knot take a four-foot length of suitable rope (AB) in your hands, and proceed as follows.

Drape end (A) of the rope over the fingertips of your left hand, as illustrated in figure one. Then put end (B) across the rope already in your left

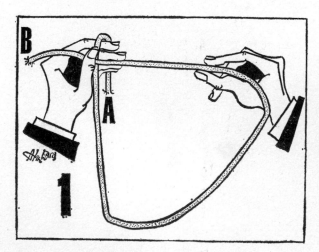

hand. Press your thumb lightly upon the rope ends where they cross. Afterwards, put your right hand outwards through the big loop and seize end (A).

Immediately pull through (A), while you let the "slack" in the loop run freely between your left thumb and forefinger (see X in figure two). As you do so, what looks like a large loose thumb-knot appears before the eyes of your audience. IT REALLY LOOKS AS IF YOU ARE TYING A GENUINE KNOT.

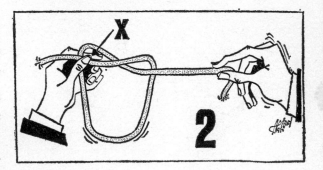

But while you pull through (A), keep your left hand higher than your right—and keep looking towards your right hand. These not unnatural actions will misdirect the attention of your audience from the way the rope is really supported by your left hand.

In fact, you don't tie a knot at all! YOUR THUMB AND FORE-FINGER MERELY HOLD THE ROPE TOGETHER TO RE-SEMBLE PART OF A REAL KNOT. So when, while the fake knot is still quite big, you part your thumb and forefinger, your audience believe they see an honest knot dissolve into nothing!

"SHOOT" A KNOT

"Can you tie a Robin Hood knot? It's really quite easy. First you form part of a rope into a 'target'. Then you pull back an end, like a bow and arrow, and finally you shoot the arrow through the 'bull's-eye' and 'score' a knot—so!"

With this simple patter, you can accompany an attractive new trick with a five-foot length of very soft, best-quality white rope. Smear Copy-

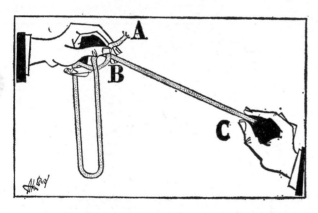

dex on the rope-ends to prevent them from fraying, then study these instructions with the rope in your hands.

Take end (A) between your left forefinger and thumb. Bring the middle of the rope up around end (A) to form a hanging loop (the target).

Alter your grip so that whilst (A) is still held fast between your forefinger and thumb-tip, the place (B) where the rope crosses itself is held firmly between the ball of your thumb and second finger.

At this stage tuck back your third and fourth fingers in order to enlarge the loop's width, to make the target easier to penetrate.

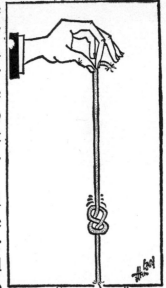

Pull back end (C) of the rope between your right thumb and forefinger. Do this as if you are aiming a bow and arrow at a target. Naturally you will be aiming at the hanging loop.

When the string is taut, let go end (C). The string's elasticity will propel it straight forward and (if your aim is true) through the target. The instant (C) passes through the loop, let all the string except end (A) fall beneath your right hand.

Then you'll be pleased to see a perfect figure-of-eight knot form and slip down towards the middle or bottom of the rope. Performed calmly (without tenseness in your hands) this little rope trick is beautiful to watch and will create much wonder and curiosity.

These two tricks may cover one of the requirements of the Gold Arrow (Entertaining) and part of the Troubadour badge ("Perform three conjuring tricks").

TIME FOR RHYME

Each of these objects rhymes with one of the others—like HAT with BAT. Put them in pairs. Now choose the one of each pair that you would use to gain a proficiency badge and name the badge.

BUTTON INITIALS

You can make a nice decoration for one of your personal belongings that is useful too by working the initials of your name in buttons.

First outline your initials in pencil or chalk; then sew small buttons—pearl buttons look attractive—over the outline.

Don't use your Cub Scout uniform for the purpose, though, will you?

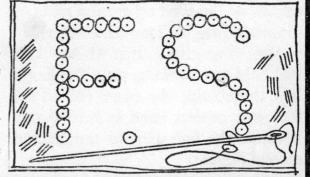

TELLTALE WEATHER SIGNS

by a COUNTRY SCOUTER

You know that "a red sky at night is a shepherd's delight", don't you? In other words, a red sky at night foretells a fine day on the morrow—and in my experience it is nearly always right.

I'm not too sure how much reliance you should place on other weather signs that many country folk swear by, but you may like to know about them and check them! Here's a long-term weather forecast well known to country men:

If the ash be out before the oak
The summer will bring heat and
    smoke.
If the oak be out before the ash
The summer will be all a-splash.

Old Ned Codlin, who has kept bees in our village all his life, insists that they are better weather forecasters than the Meteorological Office men. However clear the sky, if his bees come winging back to the hives in a hurry he declares there'll be rain pouring down in a matter of hours.

Rooks are clever forecasters. They can sense when a storm is on the way, and they drop from their high nests in the elms to fly low and tell those with eyes to see to take shelter.

Some folk believe that when cattle lie down in the meadows it is a sign that rain is on the way, the theory being that the animals are keeping a dry place for themselves; but I have not personally found this to be true. What is certain is that wild flowers like the scarlet pimpernel, the celandine and the wood anemone close their petals when moisture in the air warns them that rain is coming. It is often said that cats wash themselves thoroughly when rain is on the way. Sheep, goats and other grazing animals foretell stormy weather if they graze away from the wind and predict fine weather if they face into it.

The spider's web is, of course, a well-known weather prophet. It tightens up when rough weather is due. If you see seagulls inland, they generally bring rain with them. For fine weather they stay beside the sea. As an old rhyme says:

Seagulls, stay upon the sand;
Do not fly the rain inland.

Another country rhyme foretelling rain runs:

Fair Weather Cumulus

Showers Cumulus

Thunder Cumulus

Three days' frost and three days' fog
And rain will make the ground a-sog.

Country folk learn to read the clouds. Cirrus, or mare's-tail, clouds bring fine weather, and so do cumulus clouds, which look like lumps of cotton-wool. On the other hand, nimbus are rain-clouds; they are greyish clouds that spread all over the sky. Clouds coloured like copper bring thunderstorms, and so do "mackerel" clouds, which fleck the sky in small clouds. Showery weather follows if clouds are gathered in layers, and when distant hills seem very close this usually means that rain is not far away.

The drawings in your *Cub Scout Handbook* will help you to identify different types of cloud. For the Silver Arrow you need to know at least three types.

The moon can often tell you what next day's weather is likely to be.

An old rhyme says:
Ring round the moon,
Rain by next noon.

Cirrus Stratus

Wood Anemone

Scarlet Pimpernel

SCOUT BADGE PUZZLE

by **Rikki Taylor**

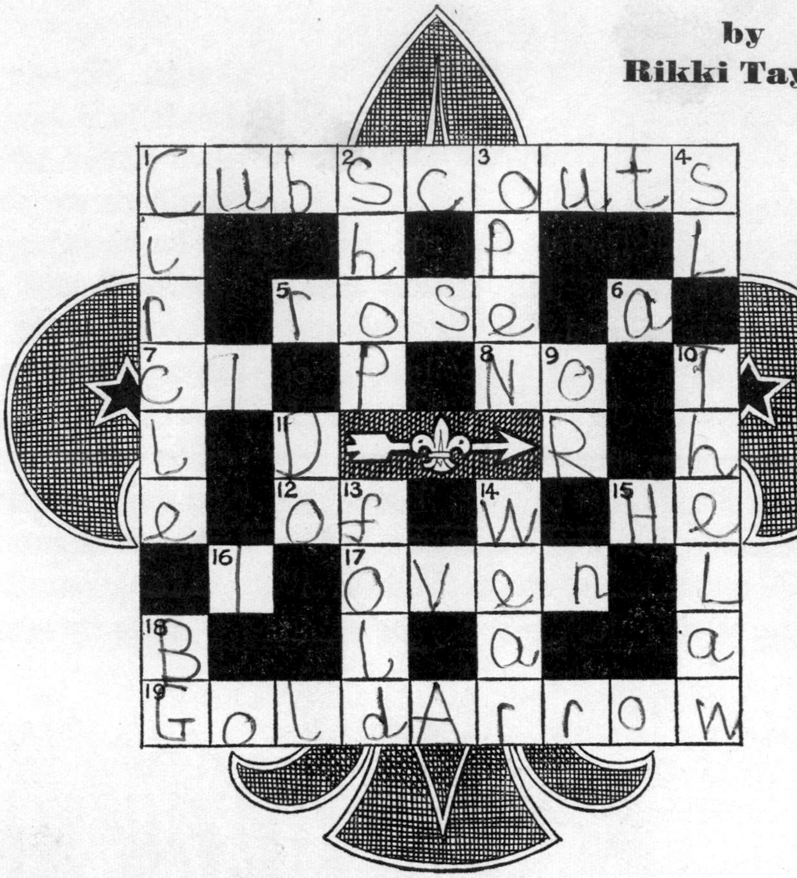

CLUES ACROSS (in brackets are the number of letters in the missing words)

1. What Wolf Cubs became in 1967 (3, 6)
5. The emblem of England (4)
7. Short for Cub Instructor (2)
8. Do you remove your *uniform* cap when the National Anthem is played? (2)
12. A Cub Scout is a member—a world-wide brotherhood (2)
15. A pronoun (2)
16. The first word of the Cub Scout Promise (1)
17. Can be made from tin or mud for camp cooking (4)
19. What every Cub Scout hopes to gain (4, 5)

CLUES DOWN

1. "Pack, Pack, Pack" makes one (6)
2. Your uniform may be bought here (4)
3. What your Group is if not connected to a church, school or other organisation (4)
4. Short for the man in charge of the Scout Troop (2)
6. The first word of the Cub Scout Law (1)
9. You may take stage A, B—C of the Handyman Badge (2)
10. Said at an Investiture (3, 3)
11. The first word of the last test for Bronze, Silver and Gold Arrows (2)
13. You do this to your uniform to keep it tidy (4)
14. You feel proud to do this with your Group scarf (4)
18. Initials of the modern "official" name for Brownies (2)

CHRISTMAS CRACKERS

CUB SCOUT: Is it hard eating soup with a moustache, Akela?
AKELA: Yes, quite a strain.

CUB SCOUT: There's a salesman outside the hall with a bald head, Akela.
AKELA: Tell him to go away. I've already got one.

BILLY: What's the difference between a Cub Scout working for a badge and a farmer tending his cattle?
SANDY: One is stocking his mind and the other minding his stock.

SANDY: Why is a pig never ill?
BILLY: Because he knows he'll be killed before he's cured.

AKELA: What did the big chimney say to the little chimney, Tony?
TONY: You're too young to smoke.

JOHNNY: What's the difference between a duck with one wing and one with two?
TONY: A difference of a pinion.

AKELA: If there are two flies on a door which would be the angry one?
JOHNNY: The one that flies off the handle.

SANDY: Who gets the sack as soon as he starts work?
BILLY: The postman.

TONY: Why does a clock look shy?
JOHNNY: Because it has its hands in front its face.

PATROL CAMP ADVENTURE

A THRILLING SCOUT STORY IN PICTURES

by LEIGHTON HOUGHTON

THE FALCON PATROL OF THE 5TH. BINGLEY SCOUT TROOP HAD BEEN GRANTED PERMISSION BY COLONEL GRICE TO CAMP IN THE GROUNDS OF CORNDEAN MANOR FOR THE EASTER WEEKEND

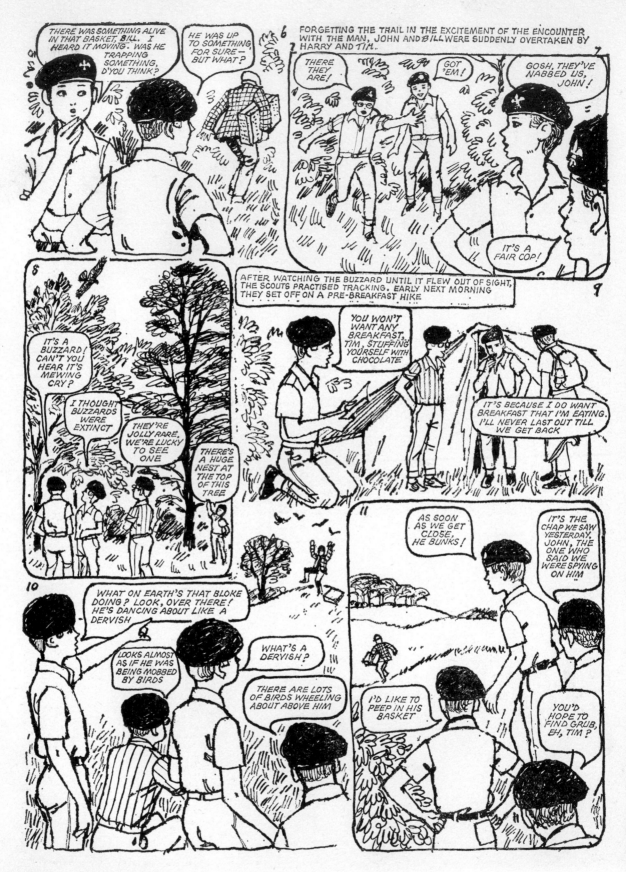

THERE WAS SOMETHING ALIVE IN THAT BASKET, BILL. I HEARD IT MOVING. WAS HE TRAPPING SOMETHING, D'YOU THINK?
HE WAS UP TO SOMETHING, FOR SURE – BUT WHAT?
FORGETTING THE TRAIL IN THE EXCITEMENT OF THE ENCOUNTER WITH THE MAN, JOHN AND BILL WERE SUDDENLY OVERTAKEN BY HARRY AND TIM.
THERE THEY ARE!
GOT 'EM!
GOSH, THEY'VE NABBED US, JOHN!
IT'S A FAIR COP!
IT'S A BUZZARD! CAN'T YOU HEAR IT'S MEWING CRY?
I THOUGHT BUZZARDS WERE EXTINCT
THEY'RE JOLLY RARE. WE'RE LUCKY TO SEE ONE
THERE'S A HUGE NEST AT THE TOP OF THIS TREE
AFTER WATCHING THE BUZZARD UNTIL IT FLEW OUT OF SIGHT, THE SCOUTS PRACTISED TRACKING. EARLY NEXT MORNING THEY SET OFF ON A PRE-BREAKFAST HIKE
YOU WON'T WANT ANY BREAKFAST, TIM, STUFFING YOURSELF WITH CHOCOLATE
IT'S BECAUSE I DO WANT BREAKFAST THAT I'M EATING. I'LL NEVER LAST OUT TILL WE GET BACK
WHAT ON EARTH'S THAT BLOKE DOING? LOOK, OVER THERE! HE'S DANCING ABOUT LIKE A DERVISH
LOOKS ALMOST AS IF HE WAS BEING MOBBED BY BIRDS
WHAT'S A DERVISH?
THERE ARE LOTS OF BIRDS WHEELING ABOUT ABOVE HIM
AS SOON AS WE GET CLOSE, HE BUNKS!
IT'S THE CHAP WE SAW YESTERDAY, JOHN, THE ONE WHO SAID WE WERE SPYING ON HIM
I'D LIKE TO PEEP IN HIS BASKET
YOU'D HOPE TO FIND GRUB, EH, TIM?

THE STRONGEST CREATURE OF ALL

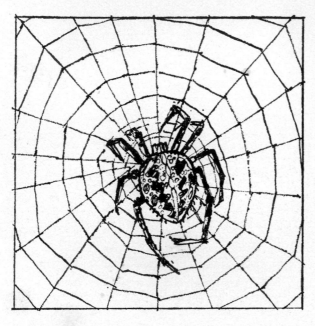

For his size the ordinary spider is the strongest and toughest living creature in the world. At the end of each of his eight legs is a pair of nippers of immense power, much stronger in proportion to size than the claws of a lion or tiger. In each of those nippers the spider can hold an insect much larger than himself, such as the daddylonglegs or even a large, fat bluebottle. Just imagine how strong a policeman would have to be to hold down eight men at once!

The spider's appetite defies all human competition. Scientists tell us that if a spider were as big as a human being he would at daybreak eat a meal equal to a small alligator, at 7 a.m. a lamb, at 9 a.m. a young leopard, at 1 p.m. a whole sheep, and the rest of his meals for the day would total up to the weight of a whole roasted ox.

As to his toughness, he can be swept from the ceiling and drop with a thud on to a stone floor and still scamper away as though he had fallen on to a bed of feathers. A drop like that would be to us like jumping from the top of Nelson's Column in London's Trafalgar Square!

"Surely you're not afraid of a spider in your tent, Billy."

BEHIND THE SCENES AT THE GANG SHOW

1

Photos by Jack Olden

1. *Cub Scouts Johnny Abbot and David Harvey go behind the scenes at the London Gang Show. All the performers belong to the Scout and Guide Movements*
2. *Johnny and David watch their Akela put on make-up before appearing in the Gang Show*
3. *"We're going to be in the Gang Show when we're a bit older," the Cubs tell a Scout "costermonger"*
4. *Johnny takes a great fancy to the Hussar uniforms worn by several of the performers*

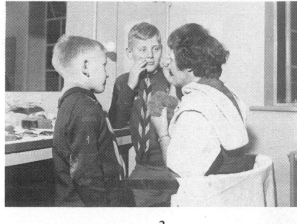

2

3

4

CUB SCOUTS OF AMERICA

by LUANNE T. RICHIE

Den Mother

Who Explains That the American Cub Scout is Like You But Different!

An American Cub Scout

The arrow points below the Wolf Badge on the pocket are awarded for completing achievements above those required to gain the Wolf Badge

During his first year, the eight-year-old Bobcat Cub Scout of America strives to earn the Wolf Badge.

Many of the things he does for the badge centre around his home and the boy himself. He may learn to whittle, organise a family picnic, climb a tree, display his collection of bugs or bottles, plant a garden, or take care of a pet.

During the second year he works for the Bear Badge. For each badge he carries through twelve separate achievements.

Be Square—Be Fair

This is what an American Cub Scout says when he makes his Promise:

"I, James Blank, promise
To do my best. To do my duty
To God and my country,
To be square and to obey
The Law of the Pack."

This American Cub Scout Promise is quite like the one made by a Cub Scout in Britain. You in Britain promise to do your duty to the Queen; we in America promise to serve our

Left to right: Cub Scout, Boy Scout, Explorer Scout. Adult supporters sponsor Scout programmes in the United States, which recently celebrated the 60th anniversary of the Boy Scouts of America

country. The added words, "To be square", mean simply to be fair to everyone at all times. Sometimes this is not easy and must be learned. A Cub Scout wants people to be fair to him, so he learns to be fair to everybody.

Some of the Cub's learning takes place at the Den Meeting, which is held every week in the Den Mother's home. The Den Mother is usually the mother of one of the Cubs.

At the Den Meeting games of all kinds are played. As well as being fun, races, relays and games help the Cubs to develop skills and to learn to be "square". One of the favourite games is called "Tails". In this, the boys tuck their neckerchieves under their belts, with about two-thirds left hanging. Hopping on one foot, each Cub tries to snatch the tails from the other Cubs' belts. The game is played in a large circle. The boys mustn't step out of line, nor put a second foot to the ground. If they should happen to break the rules, they learn to disqualify themselves and step out of the game. The winner is the one who saves his own tail and collects the most of the others'. Quite often, cookies—biscuits or cakes to you!—follow!

Den Meetings, though, aren't all games and cookies. The boys report their progress up the Wolf Trail and work together as a group. They come

The Living Circle, the ceremony that closes the Den Meeting

in full uniform, which includes blue-and-gold pants (long trousers) and shirt. They give the "V"-shaped sign and recite the Cub Scout Promise. Each Cub has a book in which he keeps a record of the skills and projects he has pursued at home. He shows his book every week to the Den Mother. On a wall-chart bearing the names of all members of the Den each achievement that his parents have signed that he has carried out is marked up. Cheers for the boy who has at last learned to do, say, a front roll may be almost drowned out by the groans of eager Cubs who haven't yet managed to do it.

The ceremony called the Living Circle closes the Den Meeting. The boys form a circle, hold out their left hands, palms down, and extend their thumbs. They clasp the hand of the boy to the left and so form a friendship ring. Holding hands, together they give the Cub Scout sign and repeat the Promise.

American Cub Scouts often work together on projects. They may get together to tidy up a vacant lot (piece of ground) or plant flowers in a public square. They also prepare something special for the monthly Pack meeting. At this meeting all the Dens in a neighbourhood, from three to eight groups, come together.

Cub Scouts Entertain

At the beginning of the year, the Pack Leaders, who are parents of the Cubs, choose a special theme for each month. Among such themes may be "Wonders of the World", "Knights of Old", and "Come to the Fair". One or two of the Dens will be asked to entertain the parents and the other Cubs with a skit or a stunt or a display that tells the story of "Wonders of the World" or "Knights of Old" or "Come to the Fair". For "Come to the Fair" the Dens might build actual country fair booths and make arts and crafts and various articles to sell at the booths. One boy might dress up as a fortune-teller at the Pack meeting, another present a ballon-dart game. Parents and boys work together.

Flag, Pledge, and Awards

Every monthly Pack meeting begins under the direction of the Cubmaster, the Pack Akela, with the presentation of the flag. This is followed by the Pledge of Allegiance. Then badges, awards and citations are made by the Awards Chairman. The parent receives the award and pins whatever it is—badge or pin—on the Cub's uniform pocket. This is always a proud moment for the Cub and for the parents who have helped him, the Denmates who have supported him, and the Cub Scout leaders who have guided him.

After refreshments, the meeting ends with the retreat of the flag, an impressive ceremony.

"Do Your Best"

Though programmes and activities in various countries may be different, the basic ideal of Cub Scouting is the same the world over. The American Cub Scout organisation was founded in 1929 and broadly follows that established by the Founder of Scouting, Lord Baden-Powell. Cub Scouts in both our countries help to further the ideal of "Live and help live". Everywhere in the world where Cub Scouting goes on boys say proudly, "Do Your Best."

Presentation of the Flag

FLY HIGH FOR GOLD ARROW

by JEAN CHAPMAN

Michael sat on a rock and watched

"We'll never be back in time now!" Michael shouted above the crash and roar of the waves. Tired and exasperated, he slumped on to a rock and watched his friend running backwards along the beach.

The kite, the cause of all the trouble, suddenly soared into the air, and just as suddenly plunged back on to the sand. Cupping his hands round his mouth, Michael shouted again.

"Steven, come on! We'll be late."

"Look," said Steven, walking back, his sandy hair sticking to his wet forehead, "I'm going to fly this kite if it's the last thing I do."

"I don't know why you bother Akela won't try to fly the thing. As long as you've made it he'll pass you for Gold Arrow Handcraft."

"He might. He's getting keen about things being done properly, and the kite has got to fly. Anyway, I don't see why this one shouldn't fly." Steven prepared to try again.

"All I know is that Akela is keen on everyone being at Pack meeting on time. If we're late again we'll lose points," grumbled Michael. "That will be our Six out of the running."

"Just let's have one more try under the cliffs. There'll be an up-current there. If I get the kite up once I shall be satisfied."

It was the beach patrol helicopter

windows, and with a derelict water-barrel at one corner. Steven was standing near the cottage wall looking up at the roof. Michael ran to him.

"I didn't know there was a house here."

"Never mind the house—look at my kite!" Steven moaned.

"Now you've had it!" Michael said. "Only a kite you'd made could find the only house for miles and wind itself round the chimney."

"If I climbed on that barrel I could reach the string," Steven decided.

Placing one foot on a rusty hoop, he heaved upwards. Once on top he could see over one corner of the roof, a bend in the cliffs, and down into a small secluded bay.

"Wow!" he gasped "I can hardly believe my eyes."

"What is it?" Michael wanted to know.

Steven held out a hand to pull his friend up.

"Gosh!" exclaimed Michael. "Look at the flag. It's a Russian ship."

"They're launching a rowing-boat. What in the world are they doing here?"

"Does anyone know they are here?"

"Well, somebody soon will. Here comes the beach patrol helicopter."

"Okay! But those cliffs are a couple of miles from the village, and the tide's coming in. One try; then if we run like mad we might just make Scout head-quarters on time."

The kite soared from Michael's hand as he held it high for the last try. Steven gave a victory whoopee as it climbed over the cliffs. Michael cried out a warning. He could see what was going to happen. The kite swung inwards to the cliff face, and plummeted out of sight.

"Why couldn't you make a bird box or something simple like that for your Hand-craft?" grumbled Michael.

"I wanted a new kite," Steven growled back, and made for the cliff. "You go if you want to. I'll be all right. There's a path here."

Michael thought of the lonely walk back along the beach and turned to follow his friend. The path was no more than a steep, rock-strewn track. Michael called for Steven to wait, but a bellow like an angry bull's was the only answer he heard. He climbed on, unexpectedly coming to a large green ledge halfway up the cliff. Nestling at the back of the ledge was an old cottage, with a black, weather-stained door set between two dirty, broken

The unmistakable whirr of a helicopter engine grew quickly louder. The helicopter swooped low over the cottage, skimmed the cliffs and was gone.

"Well," Michael exclaimed, "they ought to have seen that hammer-and-sickle!"

The two Cubs watched fascinated as the Russian sailors in their strange dark uniforms began to pull towards the beach. A line of round, black floats was dropped from the ship, and as the sailors rowed away these extended in a long, bobbing line from ship to rowing-boat.

"Do you think it's a pirate fishing-boat?"

"I'm sure they're not fishing."

The rowing-boat was dipping its bow deeply into the breakers, but landing was obviously impossible. Then both boys gasped as a sailor stood up in the bow. They had time to see a thin line coiled round his waist before he dived like a black dart into the waves.

"Unless he's a fish he'll never make the beach," Michael breathed.

A black head appeared. Then it disappeared. It appeared again, this time with an arm raised in frantic appeal.

"What's the matter? He must be nearly

on the beach. What's stopping him?"

Again the man's head appeared, then was once more swamped by the waves.

"He's in trouble. Come on!" Michael jumped from the barrel and ran.

Steven paused long enough to watch the now frantic men in the boat. Desperately the rowers bent over the oars in an effort to drive the boat through the huge breakers. Each time they drew nearer they were in peril of capsizing in the waves. They could do nothing to help their companion. The swimmer's head appeared every few moments from the breakers, only to be pulled under again and again.

Steven wasted no more time. Jumping rocks and stumbling in sudden pools of soft sand, he raced after Michael. As he reached the beach, Michael was already disappearing into the clouds of spray and foam coming from the waves as they flung themselves between beach and breakwaters.

Michael reached the man's head first, and taking his shoulders tried to lift him above the level of the water.

"It's no use," Michael called to Steven. "He must be caught in something."

"He'll drown if we don't free him. Come on!" Steven reached his friend.

Desperately, Michael tried to keep the man's head above the waves as Steven raced through the spray to help

The man gestured urgently to his left foot.

Edging deeper into the waves, Steven felt along the man's leg. He bent lower, the waves breaking over his head and shoulders as he reached downwards. His groping hands stopped suddenly. The man's ankle was tangled in thick wire cable.

This cable was obviously what the round, black buoys were carrying from ship to shore. The sailor must have become entangled as he dived from the rowing-boat.

"He's caught by the cable!" Steven shouted to Michael. "It's tangled round his foot. He'll drown if we don't move it. I'll pull at it. You keep his head up."

Time and time again Steven heaved on the cable. Soon, sobbing with effort and frustration, he realised that he and Michael could not release the man without help.

A sudden desperate idea came to Steven. Releasing the cable, he battled back to Michael.

"Keep trying to hold his head above water, Michael. I'm going to get help."

Dragging his legs through the swirling water to the beach, he headed back across the bay. Regardless of bruises and grazes, he raced over rock and boulder back to the old cottage. Unless he raced, the tide would swallow up the trapped man. In a very short time the beach helicopter would finish its patrol and return over the cottage.

Reaching the green cliff-ledge, he tore off necker, jersey and vest and jumped again on to the old water-barrel. Already he could hear the deep, steady beat of the returning helicopter. Working with desperate haste, he tied his clothes to the captive kite string. The keen wind carried them along the string, and flapped them

Frantically, Steven waved at the helicopter

in an urgent, eye-catching line against the chimney-stack.

"The pilot will see them!" Steven muttered through clenched teeth. "He must!"

The helicopter hove into view on its return trip. To Steven's anxious eyes, it seemed to be travelling much faster than usual. Swooping over the ledge and the cottage roof, it was quickly out of sight. Despair flooded over Steven. Then he heard a change in the engine note. Again the helicopter swung into view, circling swiftly over the distress-signal.

Steven almost waved his arms off with relief. There was an answering wave from the machine, and soon an overalled man swung out and down on a line. Reaching the ground, he released himself from the harness and ran to Steven.

"What's the matter, son?"

"In the little bay—a Russian sailor drowning. There's a cable round his ankle—boat can't get ashore." Steven's words tumbled over each other in his hurry to tell.

The helicopter patrolman drew in his breath sharply.

"Good lad! We'd never have seen him. We were told to keep clear and leave the Russians to work in peace. See you on the beach." He ran off, clipped on his harness again and waved an arm as he was hauled back aboard. The helicopter hurtled towards the bay.

Would the helicopter be in time? Steven ran back to the bay wondering about the trapped sailor and about Michael too. Had his friend given up trying to hold the Russian's head above the incoming tide?

As he neared the seashore, Steven saw that the helicopter crew had worked fast. Already the Russians in the rowing-boat were tying a line dropped from the heli-

A man swung out and down on a line

copter to the cable supported by the buoys. The crewman who had spoken to Steven dropped on to the beach and was now wading into the sea.

Where was Michael? Suddenly the crewman plunged below the spray and lifted a tired, gasping Cub Scout up above the waves and helped him towards the beach. Steven ran to lend a hand.

The crewman from the helicopter now battled to get the unconscious Russian seaman ashore. Slowly and steadily the helicopter pulled the line of buoys shorewards, and the crewman was able to carry the limp form to the beach.

There was a cruel gash on the Russian sailor's ankle, but now that the weight and pull of the cable was checked by the hovering helicopter, the sailor was quickly freed. Then, swiftly, artificial respiration was applied.

Steven and Michael watched, shivering in their wet uniforms. At last the Russian took a deep, shuddering breath.

The helicopter touched down on the beach. The fast-recovering seaman and Steven and Michael were wrapped in blankets and taken home, much to the amazement of their parents. They would have liked to linger to tell of their adventure, but both were bundled into bed, and the grown-ups were left to tell and hear the story.

When Pack meeting night came round again, Steven and Michael had a surprise.

"First here this week," grinned Steven, but the words had hardly left his lips when Akela popped his head round the Scout headquarters door.

"Come on!" he said. "We're waiting for you two."

"It's early," said Steven.

They both followed Akela. A tumult of cheering greeted them. The hall they had believed empty was full of people. Akela gently pushed the bewildered pair forward through Russian sailors, a helicopter crew, and Cub Scouts and their families. They were embraced, kissed on both cheeks and presented with large bouquets by the seaman they had helped to rescue.

Through an interpreter the seaman thanked the two gallant British Cub Scouts.

"We came to bring a new telephone line from Russia to England," he went on, "but you boys have made a better communication of brotherly love between two peoples of the world."

Then the Russian captain stepped forward, unpinned two medals from his own uniform and presented one to Steven and one to Michael. After pinning them on to the Cub Scouts' jerseys, he stood smartly to attention and saluted the two boys. It was the proudest moment of their lives.

"Now for the barbecue!" shouted a voice from the Cub Scout Pack.

Steven and Michael were carried shoulder-high to the beach and to the gayest, noisiest barbecue ever. When even Michael could eat no more sausages, and the Russians had given up dancing, Akela called for a Pack circle.

"One most important thing remains to be done. If Steven will come forward there is a rescued kite here and a Gold Arrow for him. I am sure we all agree that the kite flew high enough to deserve it."

Akela shook hands with Steven and then with Michael, and finally the whole Pack joined in the Grand Howl.

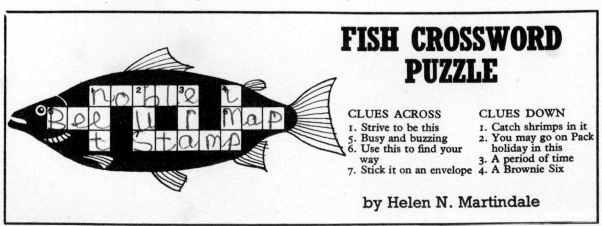

FISH CROSSWORD PUZZLE

CLUES ACROSS
1. Strive to be this
5. Busy and buzzing
6. Use this to find your way
7. Stick it on an envelope

CLUES DOWN
1. Catch shrimps in it
2. You may go on Pack holiday in this
3. A period of time
4. A Brownie Six

by Helen N. Martindale

YOUR OWN BEDROOM CLOCK

Muriel Wallington Shows You How to Make It

For Bronze Arrow (Simple Handicrafts)

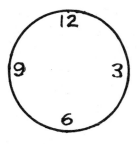
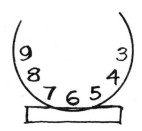

You will need the lid of a round cheese-box, a tray from a matchbox, one push-through paper fastener, a strip of coloured card, $\frac{1}{4}$" x $2\frac{1}{2}$", paints, sticky tape, and a fibre-tip pen.

Paint the box-lid and piece of matchbox in a bright colour. When the paint is dry, mark the centre of the lid and make a hole. With the fibre-tip pen write the numbers round the clock-face, with the rim facing you. It is easiest to write the 12, 6, 3, 9 numbers in the right place first of all and then fill in the others.

Snip through the rim under the 7 and 5 and then cut towards the 6 from each direction, leaving half an inch under the 6 still joined. With sticky tape join the clock to its stand. Stick the tape to one end of the matchbox-tray, with the hollow side downwards. Then pass the tape over the cut piece of rim and down the other side of the tray.

For the hands, cut the coloured strip of card into two pieces, one 1" and one $1\frac{1}{2}$" long. Cut one end of each piece to a point and make a hole in the other end. Push the paper-fastener through both hands and then through the hole in the clock and open out the fastener. You can then move the hands from the

back or at the front.

When you have made your clock you will be able to teach your younger brother or sister to tell the time.

ZEBRA AT CAMP

A True Story Told by AILSA BRAMBLEBY

Cub Scouts are used to welcoming all kinds of visitors at camp, but I very much doubt if many of us have had the fun of being called upon by a zebra! That's what happened to the 6th Salisbury Pack at their first camp by the side of a lake in Rhodesia.

When the sun was very hot the Packs had their meals on one of the shady verandahs of a large hut. One morning when everyone was busy, Terry, the Red Sixer, suddenly called out, "Gosh, look! There's a zebra!" Sure enough, approaching the hut was a fine striped zebra. It looked around with interest at the Red Six, who were making models, and at John, of the Greys, who was practising semaphore. Then two or three Cubs, with titbits in their hands, stalked gently up to the zebra to see if they could tempt him

to eat. They soon discovered that he needed no tempting.

The Cubs were delighted with their visitor—for a while! They very soon found out, however, that the zebra was a most persistent creature and that he had no idea when he had outstayed his welcome or had had more than his share of titbits. He kept turning up and pushing his way into everything that was going on —especially if it was concerned with food —till at last, when he invited himself to Dennis Maynes' birthday party, everyone felt he had gone too far!

The birthday party tea was being held on the verandah, and the Cubs were just settling down to it happily when up trotted the zebra. Dennis gave a yell, then cried, "He's not going to have my birthday cake!" Seizing it in both hands, he rushed into the hut, followed by the other Cubs— and by the zebra.

Before the zebra reached the door, however, the Cubs managed to shut it, with the cake safely on the inside.

The zebra was annoyed. He marched hungrily up and down the verandah until his eye was attracted by the Pack notice-board. He stood in front of this for a few moments, scanning it knowledgeably, and then, with strong teeth, he ripped down a notice and chewed it with relish. It was the camp menu!

At last Akela decided she must take action and persuade the zebra to return to his own home.

"But what on earth shall I drive him away with?" she wondered. "Ah, that will do!" She had spotted the kitchen fish-slice.

The last the Cubs saw of their zebra visitor was his reluctant form being driven away by Akela, who was gently but firmly waving him off with a fish-slice!

WILY WHIP WEASEL

by JEAN KENWARD

Wily Whip Weasel
Lives under the wood,
And I wouldn't mind betting
He's up to no good.
There's something odd
In the way he looks,
Like a criminal in
Detective books;
And the poor, silly rabbits
Whisper "What?
Is he a friend
Or is he not?"
Wily Whip Weasel
Gets no thinner
And he doesn't eat pudding
For breakfast or dinner.

The speed he moves at
Is quite fantastic;
Lissom and looped
Like a piece of elastic,
Smooth as treacle,
He's calculating
Who to trick next
In his hunting and hating,
Who to entice
To his bright, white trap.
"Look out!" cries blackbird.
"Watch that chap!
He's got no conscience,
He's got no shame:
Wily Whip Weasel—
That's his name."

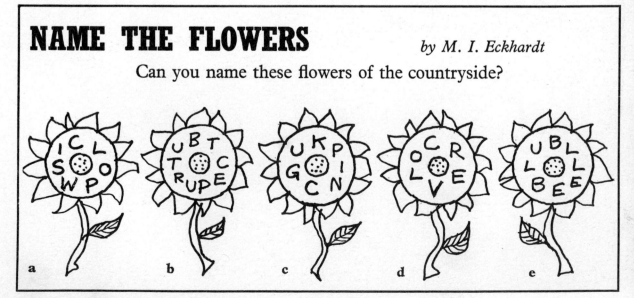

NAME THE FLOWERS

by M. I. Eckhardt

Can you name these flowers of the countryside?

a   b   c   d   e

IT ISN'T ALWAYS EASY

by Marcia M. Armitage

You know about helping others,
And duty to God is plain,
But what your duty is to the Queen
May puzzle you now and again.
You can't be one of her soldiers,
And stand on guard at her door,
Though if she knew how well you'd do it
She'd ask you to be there, I'm sure!
Perhaps if you pick up the litter
That makes a mess of the street

It would help the Queen a little bit
By keeping her country neat.
And if you see any schoolboys
Who've come from another land
The Queen would like you to help them
By offering a friendly hand.
It isn't always easy
To keep your Promise and Law,
But if you keep thinking and trying,
You'll be a true Cub Scout, I'm sure.

D

49

CALLING ALL RED INDIANS

ANNE PHILLIPS Tells You How to Make a "Hiawatha" Canoe, Wigwam and Head-dress

You've read about Hiawatha, haven't you, the Red Indian boy who lived in the mighty forests of North America and who was the hero of Longfellow's famous poem *The Song of Hiawatha*? If you haven't, you ought to make yourself acquainted with Hiawatha and what he did. *The Song of Hiawatha* is a story in verse and one that you're not likely to forget. You will probably find it in your public library, but if you can buy your own copy it will be something to treasure.

Hiawatha lived in a wigwam with his mother, Minnehaha, and his old grandmother, Nokomis. He spent much time in the forests watching the birds and animals and learning their ways.

Then the little Hiawatha
Learned of every bird its language,
Learned their names and all their secrets,
How they built their nests in summer,
Where they hid themselves in winter,
Talked with them whene'er he met them,
Called them "Hiawatha's chickens".
Of all beasts he learned the language,
Learned their names and all their secrets,
How the beavers built their lodges,
Where the squirrels hid their acorns,
How the reindeer ran so swiftly,
Why the rabbit was so timid,
Talked with them whene'er he met them,
Called them "Hiawatha's brothers".

He built himself a light birchbark canoe—
> Thus the birch canoe was builded
> In the valley by the river,
> In the bosom of the forest;
> And the forest's life was in it,
> All its mystery and its magic,
> All the lightness of the birch-tree,
> All the toughness of the cedar,
> All the larch's supple sinews;
> And it floated on the river
> Like a yellow leaf in autumn,
> Like a yellow water-lily.

To make a simple model of Hiawatha's canoe, you need a piece of brown paper or thin cardboard, longer than it is wide. If you paint it yellow, it will look like real birchbark. My piece of cardboard was 8″ long by 3″ wide.

First fold it **in half**, and then in half again. Now draw on it half of the canoe, like this—

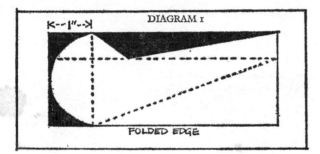

DIAGRAM 1

K--1″--K

FOLDED EDGE

Cut away the black parts and then unfold. Your canoe should now look like this—

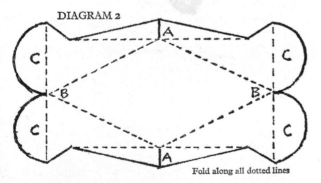

DIAGRAM 2

C   A   C
B   B
C   A   C

Fold along all dotted lines

Cut slits at A and bend along the dotted lines from A to B. Paste the two sides together at A and the ends at C. Your canoe will be nearly finished now. Make a pattern round the edges and paint a star at each end, as in *The Song of Hiawatha*—"On its breast two stars resplendent". You can float your canoe on a pool or use it as a novel container for sweets, etc.

The wigwam of Nokomis, where she nursed the baby Hiawatha, stood—

> By the shores of Gitche Gumee,
> By the shining Big-Sea-Water,
> Stood the wigwam of Nokomis,
> Daughter of the Moon, Nokomis.

Now to make your wigwam! This diagram will guide you.

You will need thick drawing-paper. Use a compass to make the semi-circle.

Before you join the wigwam together, make a pattern at the bottom with stick prints and paint it. Join the wigwam together by pasting flap A under the edge of the wigwam and flap B over the edge. Cut an oval opening for the door. Bend out the smoke-flaps, which are marked S on the diagram, and fasten

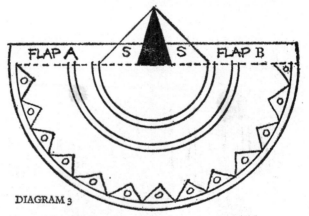

FLAP A   S   S   FLAP B

DIAGRAM 3

them with lengths of cotton or thread to some very slender cane. The wigwam will look more realistic if you have several "poles" in the middle for it to rest on.

Now add a head-dress to your Red Indian outfit.

> From his lodge went Hiawatha,
> Dressed for travel, armed for hunting;
> Dressed in deer-skin shirt and leggings,
> Richly wrought with quills and wampum;
> On his head his eagle feathers.

Ask your mother for a piece of rufflette binding, such as she uses for her curtains. Make it the right size for your head. Stick feathers into the slots. You'll soon make it look like a real Red Indian head-dress and wear it with pride.

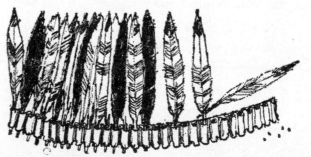

KEEPING ANTS AS PETS

by B. Clynick

Ants are fun to watch. They are even more fascinating if one can see what is going on inside their nest. This is difficult, because ants build their nests in the ground and under stones.

Why not make your own observation nest and watch them all the year round. This could start you off on the first stage of the Naturalist badge. You will find that ants are "pets" that require very little attention. Mum won't have to nag at you to clean them out or take them for a walk!

Plaster-of-paris nests are cheap and simple to make. The materials you will need are:

Plaster-of-paris.

A piece of clear glass 6ins. × 6ins.

$3\frac{1}{2}$ feet of 1 in. × $\frac{1}{2}$ in. wood.

1lb. plasticine (which can be used again).

1-inch moulding pins.

Bostik No. 1.

Vaseline.

1 small piece of fine wire gauze approx. 2 ins. × 1in.

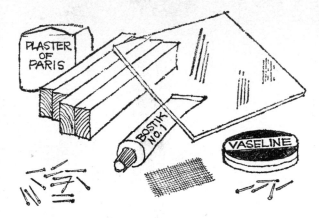

(1). Cut the wood so that you have two pieces each 7 inches long and two pieces each 6 inches long. From the wood left over, cut two more pieces each 7 inches long and keep in reserve. Using the 1-inch moulding pins, nail the four pieces together so that they fit exactly around the piece of 6 ins. × 6 ins. glass. Do not nail securely, as this is only a temporary construction. One moulding pin at each corner is sufficient. Leave the head of the moulding pin protruding a little for easy removal later.

(2). Well grease with Vaseline one side of the glass, paying particular attention to the edges. This will prevent the plaster-of-paris sticking to it.

(3). Plan roughly on paper the layout of chambers and passages for the nest.

(4). Using the plasticine, mould the shape of the chambers and passages. Make sure you allow for a feeding tunnel which can be fitted with a stopper (see diagram A). Use two pieces of wood to flatten the top and neaten the sides. When the plasticine is formed to the required shapes and

height (not less than $\frac{3}{10}$ inch, not more than $\frac{1}{2}$ inch) arrange in position on the greased glass. Make sure there is at least $\frac{1}{2}$ inch width between any chambers and passages and the edge of the glass.

(5). Shape an extra rectangle of plasticine 1 in. × $\frac{1}{2}$ in. and place on top of one of the chamber moulds. Press it

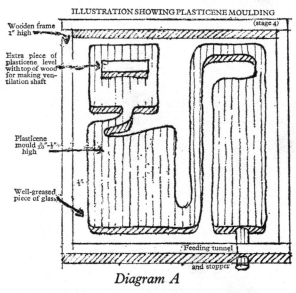

Diagram A

firmly down. The top of this piece of plasticine should be exactly level with the top of the wooden frame. Snip the four corners of the fine wire gauze diagonally for approximately $\frac{2}{10}$ inch. Fold the gauze over the top of the protruding piece of plasticine, then spread out horizontally the snipped area of gauze. The gauze will then be gripped by the plaster-of-paris. (See diagram B.)

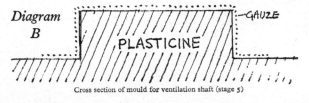

Cross section of mould for ventilation shaft (stage 5)

(6). Mix the plaster-of-paris with sufficient cold water to make a mixture that will just pour (not too sloppy). Pour over the mould. Level the mixture almost to the top of the wooden frame, being careful not to cover over the wire gauze flush with the wood. Pat down well with knife or back of spoon to ensure that the mixture fills all the cracks.

(7). Leave to set and dry for a few hours.

(8). Dismantle wooden frame, carefully remove glass and wash. Remove plasticine moulds.

(9). From one of the 6-inch lengths of wood, saw $\frac{2}{10}$ inch from its height (see diagram C). With the plaster nest the right way up, reassemble the wooden frame around it either by nailing or sticking in place with Bostik. The frame should protrude approximately $\frac{2}{10}$ inch above the plaster nest. Next, nail or stick the two reserve pieces of wood (each 7 inches long) across the bottom of the nest to hold the plaster nest in place and to allow the air to circulate underneath.

(10). Slide the sheet of glass over the top of the nest.

Now for the Ants!

Now the nest is ready. Next catch your ants!

Springtime and early summer are the best times to dig for ants. You will need a trowel, a spade, two or three plastic beakers with tight lids, an old white sheet, and an insufflator. The insufflator is a simple piece of equipment for collecting up ants. It can be made out of odds and ends (see diagram D).

Having found a nest, the first vital task is to find a fertile queen within the nest (that is, a wingless queen). In most species of ants, she is unmistakably large. Dig the nest out quickly, turning each spadeful on to the white sheet. It is easier to spot the queen against the white background. You will have to look very carefully and quickly, for the queen is skilful at hiding. If you fail to find her, turn the earth back and leave the ants to sort themselves out again. Try another nest.

If you do manage to capture a wingless queen, place her in a plastic beaker. Collect up some eggs and cocoons in another. Then, using the insufflator, collect up about two to three hundred workers.

It is extremely difficult, even impossible, to transfer lively ants to the plaster nest. There are two ways of slowing their movements. Either place the plastic containers into the fridge for about an hour (NOT the deep freeze compartment) or tip them into a bowl of tepid water for five minutes. Then pour the water through a fine sieve

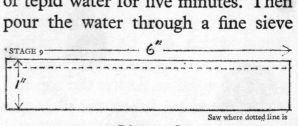

Diagram C

and shake the ants on to the nest. Cover with the glass top.

Ants need feeding only once a week; but the plaster *must* be kept damp. Suitable foods for most ants are sugar, honey, syrup, glucose solution, soft

water, and rinsed. Dead ants should be removed as frequently as possible with a pair of tweezers. Again, in order to do this it will be necessary to slow them down by cooling.

Try and borrow Grandma's large

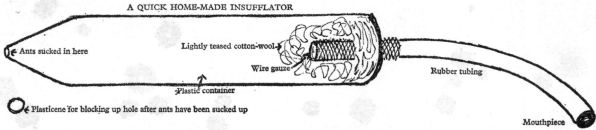

A QUICK HOME-MADE INSUFFLATOR

← Ants sucked in here
Lightly teased cotton-wool →
Wire gauze
Plastic container
Rubber tubing
Mouthpiece
← Plasticene for blocking up hole after ants have been sucked up

Diagram D

insects and a sweetened solution of meat extract. Avoid foods which go mouldy quickly.

Approximately ¼ teaspoon of food and one soft-bodied insect per week is plenty for a nest of five hundred ants. Keep a record of foods offered, accepted or rejected. Place food QUICKLY through stoppered hole.

About twice a year the nest should be washed well with warm soapy

reading-glass through which to watch your ants. You will observe many interesting habits of behaviour. You MAY observe something no one else has noticed before. Not many people study ants, and there is still a great deal to learn about them, especially about the way in which they communicate with one another.

It might be your turn one day to enrich mankind's store of knowledge!

WHAT IS THE FLAG?
asks Jean Howard

Take St. George of Merrie England
With his red cross broad and fine,
And St. Andrew, saint of Scotland—
White on blue is his design—
Then add the flag for Ireland—
It's St. Patrick's cross of red,
When you put them all together
What flag d'you get instead?
Fill in the fourth flag yourself

THE PACK

Our Pack gave a concert—admission was free,
With a nominal charge for some biscuits and tea.

The parents rolled up and then it was found
That there weren't enough forms and chairs to go round;

So the children all sat on the floor of the hall
Where, right at the front, they'd the best view of all.

The curtain went up and the concert began
With the grinning Red Six, who mimed as they sang.

Everyone clapped and the Red Sixer blushed,
Then on to the stage such a strange figure rushed.

CONCERT

by
Marcia M. Armitage

It was one of the Tawnies, dressed up as a clown.
Oh, how we all laughed when he tripped and fell down!

He did a few cartwheels and stood on his head,
Then walked on his hands. "How clever!" they said.

The Browns then, with puppets they'd made by themselves,
Gave a grand puppet show with the help of the Greys.

Just to round off the evening and do it in style
We had a camp-fire for quite a long while.

As the audience left they all said—can you guess?
That our concert had been an enormous success.

57

THREE GOOD TURNS

by NORA BLAZE

The recorder class was in full swing. "Good!" said Miss Parker. "Now try that again. One, two—"

Only Peter sat there doing nothing. He hadn't a recorder. He was one of seven children and his mother said it took her all her time to satisfy their enormous appetites and buy their clothes, never mind about recorders. She didn't seeem to realise that he had to have one. Perhaps they might manage one for his birthday, she said, but that was months away and the school concert would be over by then.

Mrs. Mason came into the classroom to put some papers on Miss Parker's desk. She was the lady who took the dinner money and added up the registers, and did things like that. She passed Peter on her way out and looked at him.

"Not playing, Peter?"

"Haven't got a recorder," mumbled Peter, red in the face.

Mrs. Mason thought for a moment, then said quietly, "Come and see me at playtime. I have an idea."

As soon as everybody rushed out to play, Peter went to the office, where Mrs. Mason sat typing a letter.

"Oh, hello, Peter!" she said, turning round. "Oh, yes, a recorder. You'd like one, wouldn't you?"

"Oh, yes, Mrs. Mason!" cried Peter fervently. "Everybody's got one except me, and Mum won't buy me one."

Mrs. Mason knew all about his family and how his dad didn't get much money working on a farm. She thought how clean and tidy they always looked and how hard Peter's mother must toil to keep them like that. There couldn't be much money to spare for things like recorders.

"Would you like to earn one?" she asked.

"Earn one?" he repeated. "You mean by running errands or chopping sticks or something?"

"No, not quite like that. Those are easy. If you can do three *special* things for me, I'll give you a recorder."

Peter's eyes lit up. He thought Mrs. Mason was super. She was kind if you forgot your dinner money on a Monday, and she always noticed if you were wearing a new pullover or anything. They all liked her.

He asked, "What sort of special things?"

58

"You're a Cub Scout, aren't you?" Peter nodded. "Then you'll be able to think of some things you can do for me. For a start, could you mend a puncture in my bike?"

"Oh, yes," he said eagerly. "I've often watched my dad mend his. You have to have a puncture outfit, though," he added doubtfully.

"Don't worry; I've got one. Will you do it after school so that I don't have to walk home?"

Peter had been looking forward to going fishing after school and nearly said so, but something in Mrs. Mason's expression stopped him. She was watching him to see if he really wanted that recorder.

"Okay!" he said. Perhaps if he mended

the puncture quickly he would still have time to do a bit of fishing, but he waited until most of the children had gone home before he got to work in the bicycle shed. He had got the tyre off and was holding it in a bucket of water to look for telltale bubbles when he suddenly felt a vicious shove in the back and pitched forward flat on his face. The bucket was knocked over as well, and all the water spilled.

"Teacher's pet! Teacher's pet!" chanted a mocking voice.

Peter picked himself up to see Garry Walters standing near him, hands in pockets, legs astride, as villains did on TV. He hated Garry, who was always taking the mickey out of him because he hadn't got roller-skates or his own bike or even a

A vicious shove in the back pitched Peter on to his face

"Silly softie!" said Garry, and kicked the tyre over the wall

recorder. Garry had everything he wanted; he only had to ask and he got it, and then he sneered at boys like Peter who had to save up or wait for things. He was big and horrible.

"Silly softie!" Garry taunted, kicking the tyre into the air and then over the school wall.

Peter was wild with fury. "You'll catch it!" he shouted, rushing up to Garry and trying to hit him. "That's Mrs. Mason's tyre. She'll think I did it."

"Pooh!" Garry pushed him off easily. He was much heavier than Peter. "Who cares about old Mason!"

"She isn't old; she's okay. She's going to — " He stopped just in time. It would never do to tell Garry why he was mending the puncture.

"Going to do what?" asked Garry curiously, but Peter dodged round him and out of the gate and fetched the tyre

back. Garry stood barring the way and caught hold of Peter's arm, twisting it behind him and hurting him. "*What's* she going to do, then?"

Peter thought fast. "She's—she's going to have to walk home if I don't mend her bike."

"Oh yeah!"

"Look, Garry," Peter said desperately, "Mrs. Mason's waiting for her bike. I *must* get on with it." He had a sudden inspiration. "Give me a hand, Garry? You hold the tyre while I— "

Garry let go of his arm and walked away in disgust, calling over his shoulder, "You must think I'm daft. I've got better things to do, mate."

Peter heaved a sigh of relief and began again on the puncture. It would be too dark now to go fishing, but at least he'd got the better of Garry for once. Dad was always telling him to stand up to bullies.

He felt quite pleased with himself and began to whistle as he worked.

Mrs. Mason was pleased, too, when she came for her bike and found it ready.

"Thank you very much, Peter. I didn't fancy walking home. Well, that's one step towards your recorder."

"What shall I do next?" Peter wanted to know.

"Ah!" said Mrs. Mason, getting ready to ride away. "You'll have to think the other two things out for yourself. The sooner you do them the sooner you will get your recorder." She rode off, smiling to herself. She had known Peter ever since the day he first came to school, a little five-year-old, clutching his dinner money.

Peter walked home, thinking hard. He wondered if he could mow Mrs. Mason's lawn—no, Mr. Mason always did that—and it would be too easy, like chopping sticks.

His mind wandered. Tomorrow, Friday, was Cub Scout night. Akela was sure to ask how he was getting on with the plant he was trying to grow from a bulb for the Silver Arrow. Peter sighed. Out of all the bulbs he had set in pots only one was really thriving. But that one was super, with purple trumpet flowers like velvet, edged with white. A gloxinia, it was called.

He was turning in at his gate now and he could see the plant on the front window-sill. It really did look great. Suddenly he tore inside, shouted "It's me, Mum!", dashed through to the front room and lifted the plant in its pot.

Mum was getting tea ready at the table. When she saw Peter carrying his plant she said, "Now where are you off to with that?"

Peter hesitated, not wanting to tell her,

so of course one of his brothers had to shout, "Bet it's for his girl friend, Mum!", making him blush and feel silly. He made for the door.

"Don't be long, wherever you're going," Mum called after him. "Tea's nearly ready."

"All right, Mum!" He was off. He knew where Mrs. Mason lived; her house was near the church. He reached it and rang the bell.

Mr. Mason answered it, and Peter thrust the plant at him.

"It's for Mrs. Mason. Will you say it's from me, please—Peter Marsden?"

"Why, yes, Peter, I'll tell her. What a beautiful plant! Wouldn't you like to give it to her yourself?"

"No, it's all right, thanks." Peter backed away shyly. "Just say it's from me and

Peter thrust the plant at Mr. Mason

that I grew it from a bulb." He turned and ran home. It had been a bit of a wrench to part with his plant, the only one he had ever managed to grow successfully, and it had taken ages to come into flower. He'd been really proud of it. Oh, well, he would start again with another. Perhaps Dad could suggest something that grew a bit quicker than gloxinias.

Mrs. Mason was delighted with her present. She called Peter as he was going into school next day and thanked him warmly. The plant was in the office window, so he could see it from the playground. He thought as Mrs. Mason was so pleased with it she might let him off the third thing, but no. She whispered, "You're nearly home and dry, Peter! Stick to it!"

He didn't see what else he could do for her. The plant had been a great idea, but what now? All through the recorder class he watched the others, longing to have one to play. He knew Mrs. Mason would keep her promise; she was that sort of person; but he couldn't think of anything else to give her. Somehow he knew that she wanted something that money couldn't buy, something that only he could give.

It was not until he was at Pack meeting that he remembered a Cub Scout wasn't supposed to take a reward for a good turn. Practising Silver Arrow knots, he wore a worried frown. Akela came over and asked if he had forgotten how to tie a sheetbend to join two ropes together. Peter looked up, surprised. He had been lost in thought.

"I know how to do it, Akela, thanks. I was just thinking."

"Something bothering you?" Akela sat on the floor beside him, and Peter found himself pouring out his problem.

"You see," he concluded, "I do my other good turns just as usual, helping Mum and all that, but this is something special, isn't it?"

Akela sat and considered seriously.

"Yes, it is," he said at last, "but look at it this way, Peter. These aren't just good turns. Mrs. Mason has promised to give you a recorder, but you have got to earn it. When you are old enough you will leave school and get a job and be paid for it, but only if you have worked well and earned the money. Good turns are for character training and very worthwhile, but this is something quite different, working for a special purpose. So don't worry about it."

"Oh, thank you, Akela!" said Peter, feeling very relieved.

"What are you going to do for your third effort?" Akela asked, getting up from the floor.

Peter had no idea.

Saturday flew as fast as usual, what with his jobs for Mum, football and playing with the gang, and then it was Sunday and best clothes and Sunday school. It was his turn to put away the hymn books, so he was the last out. Going home past Mrs. Mason's, he saw her standing at the foot of a big chestnut-tree, looking up into its branches and calling "Timmy, Timmy!" He stopped and she saw him.

"Hello, Peter!" she said. "My naughty kitten has climbed up there and now he can't get down."

Peter liked climbing trees as much as anybody, but he had never climbed one as high as this and he could see the kitten right at the top. He'd got his Sunday suit on, too. He hesitated, then took off his jacket and pullover and handed them to Mrs. Mason. She looked at him anxiously.

"Oh, I don't think you'd better, Peter. If you fell you might hurt yourself badly."

Peter wasn't very keen on the idea, either, but he didn't want Mrs. Mason to think he was afraid. "I'll be all right," he told her.

"Are you sure?"

Peter nodded and grasped the lowest branch. He pulled himself up. The bottom ones were easy, thick and strong, but when he was halfway up he saw that they became thinner and bent over frighteningly when he put his weight on them.

He looked down at Mrs. Mason and then wished he hadn't, because she looked about a mile away and he suddenly felt scared. He swallowed hard and took a firm grip round the trunk to steady himself.

The kitten mewed unhappily.

"Come on, Timmy!" he coaxed, hoping the kitten would come down to him, but it clung there.

Peter began climbing again. He kept his eyes on the kitten, but twice his foot slipped and he had to hang on grimly to a swaying branch. It's a good thing there isn't a gale blowing, he thought.

Nearly there, he held out his hand to the kitten. "Come on, Timmy! Good boy, Timmy!"

Timmy crouched on the branch and made no move. Peter edged slowly towards the kitten and managed to get a hand under the little furry body. Gently he lifted it to his shoulder, where it clung with its needle-sharp claws.

It seemed an endless climb down. Feeling first with one foot and then with the other for safe support, he climbed

"Forgotten how to do a sheetbend?" asked Akela

down and down, until at last he was on the thick lower branches. At last he dropped the last few feet to the ground.

"Peter, you brave boy!" Mrs. Mason came to take the kitten from him. "I can't thank you enough. Oh, dear, you've dirtied your nice white shirt—"

His shirt certainly was dirty, but he didn't think Mum would be cross when he told her how it had happened.

"Now," said Mrs. Mason, smiling, "I think we can go and get your recorder!"

Peter was startled. "Have I earned it?"

"You have indeed. You've done three good turns—very good turns. You mended my puncture and stood up to Garry. I saw you through the window. Then you gave me your lovely plant, which you'd grown yourself. Now you've rescued Timmy for me. Come along!" She led the way into the house, opened a drawer and handed him a beautiful shiny black recorder.

Peter eyed it in amazement. "You had it here all the time?"

"Yes! I used to play it when I was at school, and that wasn't a century ago!" She laughed. "I could have given it to you straight away, but then you wouldn't have valued it half so much, would you? And somehow I think you've learnt some useful little lessons while you've been earning it."

Peter looked up at her gratefully.

"Yes! Yes, I have, Mrs. Mason. Thank you very much."

FUN WITH PINE-CONES

by Andrew Liston

Next time you are in the country, perhaps on a Nature ramble or at camp, collect pine-cones. You can use them in many different ways.

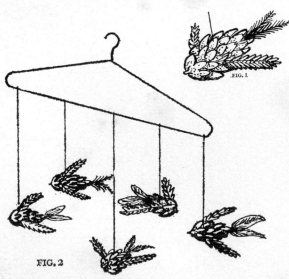

FIG. 2

Here's one way—a pine-cone bird-mobile which makes a charming and unusual decoration.

Fig. 1. Choose five large pine-cones to make the birds' bodies. They should be beginning to open out. For the wings, push an ear of wheat or a large dried grass-head into each side of the cone. Use a spot of adhesive to hold each one in place between the scales. Glue two small brown feathers or grass-heads in the point of each cone for the tail.

Fig. 2. Tie a length of cotton round each cone, then hang on a wire coat-hanger.

Now you have a fine bird-mobile.

MAKE A MULTI-MATCHBOX

A. E. IRWIN Shows You How

A couple of old Christmas or birthday cards can be put to good use in making a multi-matchbox for the home. Some cards have such nice pictures that it's a shame to throw them away. When finished, the multi-matchbox will make a nice gift for someone at home or sell readily at a Troop or Pack fund-raising sale.

Select two cards 4 in. × 4 in., or cut larger cards down to size. Back them with pieces of cardboard of the same size. Fasten them together round the edges with a passe-partout border; gold is a good colour.

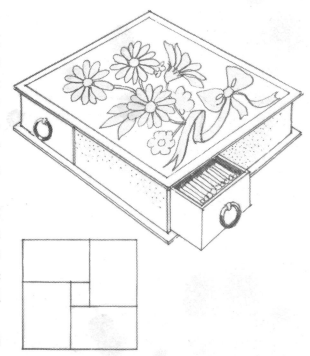

Stick them to the four matchboxes at the top and bottom (pictures facing outwards). Just before doing this, cover the ends of the matchboxes with your passe-partout paper, as shown in the sketch.

To each box a small curtain or other ring must be fixed in the centre to make it like a drawer. Rings can be secured with bits of soft metal—pieces of a large paper-fastener will do. Cut a small slit in the end of the matchbox. The piece of metal is bent round the ring, then pushed through the slit and bent down flat. A push-through paper-fastener could be used instead of a ring, if preferred.

SHOESHINE WEEK

Scout Job Week in 1972 was very much Shoeshine Week. Kits for shining shoes were sent to Scout Groups all over the country by the sponsors, the makers of Cherry Blossom shoe polish, and Scouts and Cub Scouts became busy putting a shine on the footwear of Britain's men, women and children and adding to Scout funds. The champion shoe-shiners won £30 for Group funds and £10 each to spend.

Tony is working for the Book Reader badge. Illustrated below are some of the books he has read. Can you tell from the pictures what the books are? For the Book Reader badge, Tony has to be able to tell something about three of the books he has read, show that he is able to take care of a book, prove that he knows how to use a dictionary, an encyclopaedia and an atlas, and explain how the books in a library are set out and how to find a particular fiction book.

BOOK READER

BADGE

PUZZLE

Never turn down pages

Always return borrowed books

Use a bookmark to mark your place

Handle books with care

ANSWERS

ROBINSON CRUSOE
KING ARTHUR AND THE
KNIGHTS OF THE ROUND
TABLE
ROBIN HOOD
TREASURE ISLAND

ANSWERS

HUCKLEBERRY FINN
BLACK BEAUTY
THE SWISS FAMILY ROBINSON
TWENTY THOUSAND LEAGUES
UNDER THE SEA

STAMP STOCKBOOK

W. J. Smith Shows You How to Make One

If you collect stamps and can't afford to buy a stamp-collector's stockbook, make a simple one for yourself.

You will need a few sheets of your mother's greaseproof paper, some sheets of thin card, a sharp knife for scoring the paper, and a tube of strong glue.

First cut your sheets of greaseproof paper about one inch smaller all the way round than your sheets of card. Then draw horizontal pencil-lines across the greaseproof paper about one and a half inches apart. Go over these lines with a scoring knife.

Assemble the sheets of greaseproof paper on the card and glue them on, making sure that a thin line of glue is put on directly above the cuts in the greaseproof paper. This will prevent the stamps from falling through the slots.

Once these sheets have been made up, all that remains to be done is to staple or glue them together.

TIED IN KNOTS

by Marcia M. Armitage

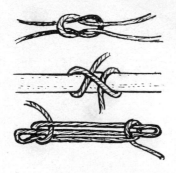

Foam-flecked waves on coral strands,
Spices brought from distant lands;
A woolly creature nuzzling grass,
Children on a slide like glass;
A relation rather out of place,
A ribbon tied with skill and grace;
Each of these images you may find
Will bring a well-known knot to mind.

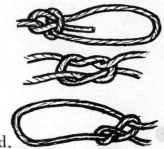

ANSWERS: Reef-knot, clove-hitch, sheepshank, slip-knot, granny knot, bowline.

CONTRIBUTIONS

Contributions to the *Sixer Annual* are welcomed throughout the year. They *must* be accompanied by a stamped and fully addressed return *envelope*. Address to the Editor, Scouting/Guiding Annuals, Purnell/Bancroft Books, P.O. Box No. 2LG, St. Giles' House, 49/50 Poland Street, London, W.1.

WISE WORDS

Failure is not falling down. It is remaining there when you have fallen.

The wishbone keeps you going after things, the jawbone helps you ask the necessary questions to help you find them, and the backbone keeps you at it until you get them.

THE COMPASS GAME

This game will help you to memorise the points of the compass. You need two players, two packs of cards, and some buttons for counters.

Shuffle the cards and place them face downwards; then take it in turns to draw a card. If you pick an Ace, a King, a Queen or a Jack you place a button on a circle of the same suit—that is, a Heart on a Heart, a Club on a Club, a Diamond on a Diamond, a Spade on a Spade. Thus, if you draw the Ace of Spades you place your button on N or NNE or NE or ENE.

Cover All Points to Win

The first to cover up all points of the compass wins. If when you reach the end of the pack all the points are not covered, reshuffle the pack and go on drawing again.

LOOKING AFTER ZOO ANIMALS

by a Keeper

"You're tickling me pink!" grunts London Zoo's panda, Chi-Chi, as he gets his tummy brushed

If you visit a zoo when you are finding out about wild animals for the Naturalist badge, you may think that you'd like to work in one when you grow up. With so many different animals to look after there is always plenty of work and some very unusual jobs to be done.

Perhaps you would like the job of giving the alligators a spring-clean. During the winter months they lie sleepily on the bed of their pool and get covered in mud, foliage and queer bits and pieces that collect in the grooves of their tough hides. When the pool has been drained one keeper turns the hosepipe on, while another scrubs the alligator's broad back with a stiff broom.

Another hard but worthwhile job is polishing up the giant tortoises. First the dust must be rubbed off, then the shell wiped over with pig-oil, and finally polished up till you can see your face in it. The tortoise may not think much of its spring-clean, so it's wise to keep away from its head end,

"This is what I call getting well oiled," says Speedy, a giant tortoise at Belle Vue Zoo, Manchester, as he gets his annual oil-and-polish

but the colours of the shell will come up beautifully when it is finished.

But perhaps you will prefer to groom the elephants. Every day they must be given their brush-up and shower, for they pick up a lot of dust and dirt when they roll over on the ground. Sometimes their nails may need filing, and this is done with a giant rasp and sandpaper.

The lions are very sleepy in the mornings, but most of the animals are ready for their breakfast early, especially the mountain goats, who hardly ever seem to sleep. So are the monkeys, sea-lions and camels.

Some of the tamer lions much appreciate having their manes combed through and look very proud of themselves when their toilet is completed.

If it is cold weather the "chimps" welcome a nice hot cup of tea for their "elevenses". At night their keeper will sometimes hand them a few hot potatoes to use as hot-water bottles, though before morning they have often disposed of their "bottles" in quite a different way!

The bears must have more bread and vegetables during the winter, when they cannot depend on their large public to supply them with tit-bits.

The teeth of the apes have to be brushed daily. Sometimes the baby monkeys have trouble in cutting their teeth, so they may be given a broom-handle to "cut" their teeth on.

Yes, it's all in the day's work if you fancy being a keeper.

"Just where I itched!" rumbles this Whipsnade Zoo rhino, as he enjoys his wash-and-brush-up-with-manicure

TREE

When you're hiking through the woods you probably like to see the living, green trees, the oaks, birches, and pines. Usually no one pays much attention to the old, hollow trees, except to chop them down.

If you did spot a hollow tree, you might see the bleached, silver-grey wood stripped and peeled by the wind, rain and snow. And you might think the tree had lost its beauty and use-fulness.

But look closely at the base of the trunk. See the fresh wood chips? They are a very good sign that this dead tree still provides a home for some lively forest creatures.

A hole at the base of the trunk may be the entrance to a badger's sett. Perhaps he and his sow are at this moment fast asleep underground among the deep roots.

Another hole round the back could be a rabbit's back exit.

Look closely at the side of the trunk and up about ten feet or so and you might see a burned and charred, oddly shaped hole. This is pretty good evidence a bee-hunter tried to smoke out a swarm of bees to collect their honey.

Walk closer to the grey trunk shell and examine the countless tiny round holes busy insects have made. You may even see long, even scratches on the trunk made by the badgers' claws.

Want to see how alive this hollow tree really is? Well, just take a com-

SECRETS

by Anthony Joseph

fortable seat on the ground near by and move nothing but your eyes. Animals can sense the least bit of unusual movement in the woods, and they'll wait until everything is quiet before they show themselves.

After ten or fifteen minutes of silent, motionless study don't be surprised to detect movement from a lofty perch or knot-hole. A squirrel has decided to come out and sun himself; or out from one of the many trunk holes a woodpecker may poke its crimson head.

Woodpeckers use their sharp-pointed beaks to drill and chisel through the outer trunk to capture insects and make a nest. Their *rap*, *rap* hammerings echo through the forest and can hardly be mistaken.

Maybe, nearer dark, you'll even hear an owl hoot from the darkness of one of the holes in the upper trunk to show that he's guarding his hollow-tree home.

As long shadows fall and streak across the forest floor, be ready for more movement. Depending on how much patience you have to watch, you might just see a colony of bats slip noiselessly out from an upper branch for a night's flight and feeding. They return before sunrise to sleep in the hollow trunk, where they hang upside down by their claws inside.

When you're ready to leave, mark your hollow tree for another secret visit. You may want to return soon.

Reprinted by permission from the *Christian Science Monitor*.

PARDON MY FROGSPAWN

by LIZABETH SLEEP

"I wonder if there's any frogspawn down there." Oliver Crumb knelt on the bank of the pond and blinked short-sightedly through his round, rimmed glasses. "I'd like to have some tadpoles. Tadpoles are interesting. I've got an uncle

Oliver held out a handful of frogspawn to David

who's an anthro—anthro—who studies animals, and he started with tadpoles. I might want to be an anthro—like him when I grow up."

"It's very muddy down there," David objected.

Oliver Crumb looked at him over the top of his glasses. "Mud will wash off."

"And we haven't got anything to put them in," David pointed out.

"We've got pockets," Oliver Crumb explained patiently. "That's what pockets are for—for putting things in."

David followed him slowly and care-fully down the steep bank. He was already late home from Pack meeting. His mother would be annoyed if he arrived home with mud all over his Cub Scout uniform.

By the time he reached the water's edge Oliver Crumb was already crouching in the thick black ooze.

"There's some!" Oliver reached out through the long weeds and pulled out a slimy handful. He pushed it, dripping with water, into a pocket of his Cub Scout shorts. He took another handful and pushed that into his other pocket, adding a little wet pond weed for good measure. He looked up at David. "I'll get some for you now," he offered generously. Reaching out, he grabbed two more slippery hand-fuls and held them out to David. "Put

74

Trying to avoid Oliver, David stepped back, missed his footing, and fell into the pond

it in your pocket," he ordered.

"I don't think I'd better," David said. "My mother goes on about things like that. I'll carry it in my hands."

"We'd better get it home quickly," Oliver said. "Frogspawn ought not to be out of the water for too long. My uncle told me." He started to climb back up the steep bank and then turned and looked over his shoulder at David. "You'll never climb up here with your hands full. Wait until I reach the top and I'll pull you up." He scrambled on and was almost at the top of the bank when his foot slipped and he came sliding down again.

David, forgetting the water behind him, took a hasty step backwards to avoid his friend, missed his footing and fell into the pond. The water, though not deep, was deep enough to soak him and his clothes, and the bottom of the pond was thick with black mud that had a most unpleasant smell.

As he sat up, he saw Oliver Crumb staring at him in surprise. "What did you do that for?" Oliver asked. "I thought you didn't want to get dirty. Fancy making all that fuss about not putting frogspawn in your pockets and then jumping in the pond and getting all your clothes wet."

"It was your fault!" David glowered as he spat out a mouthful of pond weed.

"My fault!" Oliver Crumb was indignant. "It couldn't have been my fault. I never even touched you."

David spluttered speechlessly. It was always the same. Things always went wrong when Oliver Crumb was around and he always said that it wasn't his fault. He looked at Oliver through narrowed eyes. Sometimes, just sometimes, he wished that Oliver Crumb wasn't his best friend.

"Oh, give me a hand!" he sighed.

Oliver rushed forward helpfully. He reached out, seized David's hand and heaved. He heaved so hard and so suddenly that David was dragged forward

75

and ended up flat on his face in the water.

"Well, you can't blame me this time," Oliver Crumb said with some satisfaction. "You told me to give you a hand."

For a brief second David lay where he had fallen. When he lifted his head, Oliver was kneeling beside him at the water's edge.

"If you're drowning," Oliver said hopefully, his blue eyes gleaming through his glasses, "I'm very good at artificial respiration."

David ignored him, sat up and began to grope about under the water. "My shoe! It's gone! It must have come off when you pulled me."

"I wish you'd stop messing about in that pond." Oliver frowned as he patted his pockets. "I want to go home and get my frogspawn into water."

"Well, I can't go home without my shoe," David snapped.

"It must be there somewhere," Oliver said impatiently. "I'd better help you find it. I'm very good at finding things." He searched along the bank until he found a long, sharp-ended stick. Leaning forward, he began to jab it hard into the water round David's feet.

"Ooch!" David leapt into the air, clutching at his shoeless foot, and almost fell over again. "That was my toe you jabbed!" He glared at Oliver, snatched the stick from his hand and began to prod the mud himself.

Half an hour later he was still prodding. He was also very wet and shivering with cold. It was beginning to grow dark too.

"I'll have to go home without it," David muttered.

He pulled his feet from the oozing mud and climbed slowly out of the pond. He squelched along the road with his Cub Scout uniform leaving a dripping trail of

David felt the ladder beginning to rock

strong-smelling mud behind him.

"It's jolly uncomfortable walking with only one shoe on," he complained.

"Why don't you take it off, then?" A faint gleam began to appear in Oliver Crumb's eyes. "It would be much easier for you to walk without it. I could borrow it to put my frogspawn in. I don't think it's good for the frogspawn to be in my pocket for such a long time." He looked reproachfully at David.

"You're not putting frogspawn in my shoe." David limped on.

"I've got an uncle who's a chiropodist," Oliver Crumb said thoughtfully. "He says it's good for people to walk about without shoes—without both their shoes," he added quickly.

"I don't care what your uncle says," David muttered. "You're not having my shoe for your rotten frogspawn. Anyway, I thought you said that your uncle was an anthro—something—studies animals."

Oliver Crumb looked at him severely over the top of his glasses. "I've got a lot of uncles," he said firmly. "I've got another one who's an inspector for the R.S.P.C.A. and he says that I ought to report people who are cruel to animals, and tadpoles are animals."

"You're still not having my shoe for them." David limped on as his home came into sight. "I don't know what my mother's going to say. I know there'll be a row about me coming home late and losing my shoe. When she sees my uniform all covered in mud, she'll go mad."

"Why don't you creep in and change out of your uniform?" Oliver Crumb suggested. "You can give me your wet uniform and I'll get my mother to dry it for you."

The wet bundle dropped over Oliver's head

"That's a good idea." David stopped and stared at him.

"Yes, it is," Oliver Crumb agreed modestly.

"There's a ladder in our garden shed," David told him. "I could get it out and climb up through my bedroom window."

Oliver Crumb stood on the bottom rung of the ladder to hold it steady as David climbed up. David pushed open the window, scrambled through and heaved a sigh of relief.

He was shivering badly as he stripped off his wet uniform and rubbed himself dry. Even when he had dressed he still felt so cold that he could hardly keep his teeth from chattering. He gathered his wet uniform into a bundle and peered out of the window at Oliver, who was still standing on the bottom rung.

"I'm coming down now," he called softly.

He dropped the bundle from the window, swung his legs over the sill and began to climb down the ladder. He had only taken a couple of steps when the ladder began to rock. He turned his head and looked down. The wet bundle he had dropped had fallen over Oliver Crumb's head, and Oliver, holding onto the ladder with one hand, was trying to dislodge the bundle with the other. As he twisted and turned, the ladder swayed precariously.

David clung to it tightly. "Leave the clothes alone," he called. "Let me get down first."

"It's all right." Oliver Crumb's voice was muffled. He had managed to pull the shorts away from his head but the wet jersey was still entangled round his face. "I've almost got it off."

He tore the jersey away from his eyes with one last heave that brought one side of the ladder swinging round.

"Push it back against the wall," David yelled. "Push it . . . !"

When he opened his eyes again there was a pain in his leg. His mother was bending anxiously over him. "Now you lie down," she said. "I think your leg may be broken and I don't want you to move. I'm going to phone for the doctor now."

Oliver Crumb took her place at David's side, his blue eyes gleaming hopefully. "I'm very good at first-aid," he said. "I've got an uncle who's a doctor. He taught me. Would you like me to look at your leg?"

"Don't you touch it!" David struggled to sit up. "I know what you're like. You'd probably break it right off!"

Oliver looked disappointed and then his face brightened. "I hid your uniform," he said. "Your mother doesn't know about it. And isn't that lucky?" He nodded at David's leg.

"What's lucky about a broken leg?" David moaned.

"If it's broken," Oliver Crumb explained, "you'll have it set in plaster. The plaster will come right over your foot. You won't need to wear a shoe, so your mother won't notice that you've lost it." He looked over his shoulder as David's mother came hurrying back. "I'd better go now," he said.

He was round at the back of the shed collecting David's wet uniform when he heard the doctor arrive.

"It's broken all right," he heard the doctor say. "I'd better have him in hospital for a few days."

Oliver Crumb picked up the rest of the uniform thoughtfully. It was a pity that David was so clumsy. Fancy falling into a pond twice and down a ladder too! Things like that always seemed to happen to him.

He picked up the remaining shoe and stared at it thoughtfully. David wouldn't need any shoes at all in the hospital. A slow smile dawned on Oliver's face and his blue eyes gleamed. Gently he turned out his pockets and slid the frogspawn into the shoe. "I don't want anything to happen to my tadpoles," he muttered, as he carried them carefully down the road.

RIDDLE-ME-REE

by Helen N. Martindale

My first is in cold but not in hot,
My second's in lamp but not in torch,
My third is in mop but not in top,
My fourth is in pan but not in scorch,
My whole is somewhere you may have been—
Cub Scouts go there when they're really keen.

A FISHY TALE

— DODSWORTH —

"Been fishing long, sir?"

GOD SAVE THE QUEEN!

Jane Willis Tells You Interesting Facts About the National Anthem That Will Help You with Bronze Arrow

One of the requirements of the Bronze Arrow is that you should learn the National Anthem and know how to behave when it is played in public. Here are some facts about the National Anthem that many people don't know.

The tune of the National Anthem has been "top of the pops" for more than two hundred years. After the final defeat of Bonnie Prince Charlie at the Battle of Culloden in 1745, a patriotic hymn was sung at Drury Lane Theatre, London, entitled "God Save Our Lord the King". It was also published in the *Gentleman's Magazine* as a song for two voices, but no one really knew who wrote the tune or the words, and they still don't to this day! It was sung by Henry Carey, who composed "Sally In Our Alley", and he claimed to be the author of the words and composer of the music; but it is thought that he only arranged and adapted a version that was written by Dr. John Bull, who was organist and composer to Queen Elizabeth and King James I.

A feeling of national pride was sweeping across the country, and "God Save the King" was adopted as the National Anthem. From that time it has been used on all state and royal occasions.

Just as most countries have a flag to fly, so too they have a national song. Most of these anthems proclaim devotion to a king or queen, but during the French Revolution, after the French king had lost his throne, national anthems changed and were sung in praise of freedom and the people of republics that had neither king nor queen. The French national anthem is called *La Marseillaise*. That of America is *The Star Spangled Banner*.

Many famous composers have used the tune of God Save the Queen in their work, Haydn, Brahms and Beethoven among them.

CUB SCOUT ARCHERS

Photos by Harry Hammond

Cub Scouts of the 3rd Collier Row Group, Chingford, Essex—which has an archery club, the Lone Pine Bowmen—take the first steps in learning to become Robin Hoods

Under the watchful eyes of the Group Scout Leader and his expert Scout archers, Cubs learn to remove arrows from the target without damaging them

Scouts of the Lone Pine Bowmen Club demonstrate how it should be done

A SILHOUETTE PORTRAIT GALLERY

For Your Six Den

Suggests Keith Pennyfather

You can very easily make a set of silhouettes of your Six and other members of your Pack.

Pin or fasten a fairly large sheet of paper to the wall, about four feet above the floor, and fix up a fairly strong light—a table-lamp without a shade is ideal—some distance from the wall, say about four to six feet, according to the power of the lamp.

Now invite one of your Six to pose as a "model". Ask him to sit on a chair about a foot away from the wall between the paper and the lamp. Make sure he is facing sideways—that is to say, see that he's looking *along* the wall and not *towards* it.

Take a pencil (preferably a soft one—a B or 2B, for instance), and when the Cub's shadow is in focus on the wall draw round the outline on the paper. You may have to move the lamp backwards and forwards a little before the edges of the shadow appear sharp enough.

All that remains now is for you to blacken the centre of the silhouette with crayon or Indian ink; then the job is finished.

Make silhouette portraits of others in your Six and Pack, and ask another Cub to make *yours* while *you* sit on the chair.

You could put your silhouette gallery on display in the Den on special occasions. You might run a profitable stall at a bazaar or fete too, charging, say, 2½p for visitors to have their silhouette portraits drawn.

CARING FOR YOUR PETS

by PHYLLIS BRIGGS

If you own a pet you could make a good start towards gaining the Naturalist badge, which requires you to know how to look after a pet properly.

It means a lot to your pet if, besides loving it, you try to understand it and train it and treat it properly. It is more than hard on your puppy if, after romping joyfully all afternoon, you rush in to your tea and forget that it too would like something to eat. You are saying, of course, that no one could possibly forget such a thrilling task. But after the excitement of first owning a pet has worn off, it is easy to overlook its needs.

But let's pretend that it is the first day and that your kitten or puppy has just been picked out of its travelling basket and is looking round nervously at what seems to be a crowd of terrifying new giants. Be firm, and insist that there must be no scrambling to cuddle it. Ask the others to go out of the room and give it time to calm down a little. It will probably be too upset to eat, but don't worry. Provide it with a cosy

basket and in the case of a kitten add a tin tray with sawdust, and see that drinking water is *always* where your pet can get it. Change the water at least once a day.

If it won't eat, be patient. Put something where it can get it and don't flurry it. I remember a half-wild kitten of mine which rushed under the kitchen dresser as soon as it was released and stayed there cold and hungry all the first night, despite my coaxing. In the morning it had calmed down, and strutted out to explore and have a hearty breakfast. If I had moved the dresser or tried to pull the kitten out I might have hurt it.

It is mistaken kindness to give your dog or cat something to eat which is not good for it, just because you like it yourself and want to share your treat. You may think it will love cracking up the chicken or rabbit bones from your plate, but the dagger-like splinters can harm it or even kill it. Veal bones and pork bones are safe and so are big beef bones, but avoid mutton bones.

Your cat may look wistfully at your fried plaice, but be firm and do not put down the bones and all those edging bits, brown and brittle. See that puss gets its fish, but take the bones out first. Cats adore variety. If you were to give a cat minced chicken or salmon for every meal, every day, it would soon turn away in disgust and go out to turn over some rubbish-heap in search of a change.

But cats and dogs do need meat. It is, after all, their natural food and they should have it as well as biscuit and vegetables. The old-fashioned diet of endless bread and milk for the cat will not result in a healthy pet with a good glossy coat. Some cats have peculiar fads for foods which you might think unnatural. One cat I knew would turn away from the most tempting fish if you put down a saucer of real egg-custard. Another had a passion for stewed mushrooms. Commonsense, rather than hard and fast rules, is needed.

A good tip with persian kittens is to mix a drop of hot water with their milk. The warm, slightly diluted drink is better for them and they will soon

love it and refuse cold, full-cream milk.

Dogs, we know, love exercise and they must have it. You may be cosy by the fire with a book, but if it is time for Bouncer's little run, then take it out. That is part of your duty to your dog to keep it fit and happy. Groom your dog daily with a proper dog-brush, one with a strap to fit over the back of your hand. Be very careful when brushing its head, and mind its eyes.

Cats, of course, do their own exercising. But unless your cat asks to go out at night don't push her out

into the cold on going to bed.

Perhaps instead of a cat or dog, you have rabbits as pets. The rule for exercising extends to them too. Once a day at least they must be let out of their hutches to stretch their paws on the lawn, or, if it is cold and wet winter weather, then in a dry shed or outhouse. Keep the hutches very clean. Rabbits cannot live on lettuce alone, as some people seem to think. Oats, oatmeal, split peas, an occasional carrot, bread-and-milk, bran, roots, cabbage-leaves and many other things will be good food for them. The pet-shop where you buy the foodstuff will tell you how much to give them and how to prepare the meals.

Your pets will be happier if you make them obey a few simple rules instead of being allowed to do just as they please. Insist on no jumping on the table. Never allow your pet to sleep on your bed. Teach your dog to walk always at your left side—but don't smack it if it doesn't pick up the idea at once. Remember it is trying to understand and please you, but it can't always make out at once what you want.

Lastly, never go away for a holiday trusting someone you don't know well to look after your pet every day. Unless you know by experience that the friend is absolutely trustworthy, look out for some reliable dog and cat kennels where they will care for your pet while you are by the sea.

Owners of animals don't always understand that pets like and need company. Loneliness can be as frightening to a puppy or a kitten as to a little boy or girl. It isn't enough to leave a pet with food and drink for a weekend; it needs company, affection and care as well.

EXCITING NEW
£100 PRIZE COMPETITION

You could win a superb new CASSETTE RECORDER of the latest type, worth £50, or something else of equal value, like a bicycle, a transistor radio, a record-player, or a fully automatic camera, in this simple and interesting competition. As well as your personal prize, you will also win £50 for your Pack!

When you have read your *Sixer Annual*, choose what you think is the best and the next best story, article, puzzle, etc. in each of the six groups printed below, then say in not more than about fifty words what you like most about the *Sixer Annual*.

The double prize will be awarded to the entry that exactly or most nearly agrees with the one the Editor has marked up and that has the most interesting write-up.

GROUP 1 (STORIES)
A Strange Flight
B Fly High for Gold Arrow
C Three Good Turns
D Pardon My Frogspawn
E SOS – Emergency
F Splashdown for the Black Six
G Mike's Good Turn
H Zebra at Camp

GROUP 2 (ARTICLES)
A Keeping Ants as Pets
B Looking After Zoo Animals
C Caring for Your Pets
D Cub Scouts of America
E God Save the Queen
F Telltale Weather Signs
G Collect Shells and Seaweed
H Are Both Eyes Open?

GROUP 3 (EDITOR'S PAGES)
A Your Favourite Tree?
B They Flew for Freedom
C The Editor's Chat

GROUP 4 (PUZZLES)
A Rope Tricks
B Time for Rhyme
C Scout Badge Crossword Puzzle
D Book Reader Puzzle
E Tied in Knots
F The Compass Game
G Laddergrams
H Name Tim's Dog
I Lost in London
J Picture Jigsaw

GROUP 5 (THINGS TO MAKE)
A Bedroom Clock
B Calling All Red Indians
C Fun with Pine-Cones
D Multi-Matchbox
E Stamp Stockbook
F Silhouette Portraits
G Indoor Garden
H Grow Mistletoe

GROUP 6 (VERSE)
A O, Little Town of Bethlehem
B Wily Whip Weasel
C It Isn't Always Easy
D The Pack Concert
E Song of a Cub Scout

THE SIXER ANNUAL NEW COMPETITION ENTRY FORM

Just write down the letter that is set against the title of your choice in the list above

GROUP 1 (STORIES)
BEST ....
NEXT BEST ....

GROUP 2 (ARTICLES)
BEST ....
NEXT BEST ....

GROUP 3 (EDITOR'S PAGES)
BEST ....
NEXT BEST ....

GROUP 4 (PUZZLES)
BEST ....
NEXT BEST ....

GROUP 5 (THINGS TO MAKE)
BEST ....
NEXT BEST ....

GROUP 6 (VERSE)
BEST ....
NEXT BEST ....

MY NAME IS ....

MY ADDRESS IS ....

MY AGE IS .... MY PACK IS ....

MY AKELA'S NAME AND ADDRESS IS ....

....

THE SIXER ANNUAL
NEW £100 PRIZE COMPETITION

The *Sixer Annual* double-prize competition last year was so popular that the publishers are inviting you to enter another one this year.

The competition gives an equal chance to every Cub Scout, whatever his age.

Not only can you win a fine cassette recorder for yourself, but £50 for your Pack as well, to spend just as they decide. If you prefer something else of equal value to the recorder, the choice is yours.

You have plenty of time to enter, so read and enjoy your *Sixer Annual* from cover to cover without rushing through it. Then, when you have decided which of the various contributions in each of the groups printed overleaf you like best and next best, fill in the entry form and then write down in your own words in the space below what you like most about the *Sixer Annual*.

When you have completed both front and back of the entry form, cut it out and put it, unfolded, in an envelope addressed to THE SIXER ANNUAL NEW COMPETITION, PURNELL/BANCROFT BOOKS, 49/50 POLAND STREET, LONDON, W.1.

Your entry must arrive not later than March 31st, 1973. The result will be published in the monthly magazine *Scouting* for June, 1973.

The publishers' decision is final, and no correspondence will be entered into in connection with the competition.

Good luck to you!

What I like most about the Sixer Annual

IT'S SNOW GOOD

A Short Short Story by EILEEN CHIVERS

At the Cub Scout Pack meeting there was thick snow upon the ground. The Cubs had great fun snowballing each other before going inside for their meeting.

During the meeting the Cub Scout Leader told them that the snow gave them an opportunity for doing a special good turn. He asked if anyone knew what it was, and Barney's hand immediately flew up.

"We could sweep away the snow from the old people's paths," he suggested.

"That's exactly what I thought," replied Akela. "Before we go home I shall give you the addresses of old people living alone, and tomorrow you can go along in twos and clear their paths for them."

The next day Barney and his friend Monty went along with brooms and shovels to the address they had been given.

They were getting along very nicely with the snow-clearing when the front door opened and a boy came out. He said, "Thanks for doing that. Mum said I had to do it."

The Cub Scouts then realised that this was the wrong house! They soon found the right one, and the boy, whose name was Peter, went along and helped them.

They all had a good laugh over it whilst they drank delicious hot cocoa, which Peter's mother made for them.

A Cub is a boy with a jersey of green,
With mud on his knees, and his hands none too clean.
Though words cannot hurt him, clean water might
If he's made to wash daily, both morning and night.
But he'll say, "Hip-hooray
For the fun and the friendship of Cub Scouts today!"

SONG OF

(to the tune *Willikins and His Dinah*)

He likes the team spirit a Cub Six instils;
He has help and instruction in learning new skills.
He's an armful of badges, which prove he can do it
(At least that's his story, and he's sticking to it)!
And we say, "Hip-hooray
For the fun and the friendship of Cub Scouts today!"

In Job Week he works to earn funds for his Pack.
He'll spit and he'll polish, he'll sweep and he'll stack;
He'll run all the errands and push out the pram,
And he'll whistle and grin, if requested to "scram".
And he'll say, "Hip-hooray
For the fun and the friendship of Cub Scouts today!"

A CUB SCOUT

by **SHEILA DEFT**

Cub tries to do a good turn every day.
tries in his work and he tries in his play;
tries when help's needed; he tries when it's not,
he's sometimes the most trying boy of the lot!
he'll say, "Hip-hooray
the fun and the friendship of Cub Scouts today!"

A Cub will grow up into manhood some day,
With his Law and his Promise still pointing the way.
For honour and courage and friendship he stands,
And the world of the future is safe in his hands.
And he'll say, "Hip-hooray!"
For the Scouters who've taught him and shown him the way.
Yes, he'll say, "Hip-hooray!"
For the Scouters who've taught him and shown him the way.

SOS · EMERGENCY

by **SYBIL JOSTY**

The two walked home gloomily

Simon, Sixer of the Greys, was walking home with his friend Mark from the weekly Pack meeting. Rather glumly, a frown on his freckled face, he said: "It's not so good on Fridays now, is it?"

Mark shook his head. "It's Jem," he said, coming straight to the point. "He's always stirring up trouble."

"I wish he hadn't joined our Pack," rejoined Simon. "He pushes the smaller boys around."

"He doesn't try for any badges, either. Says it isn't worth while. Why does he come? That's what I'd like to know."

"Goodness knows!" Then Simon's usual cheerful expression returned. "My brother John's going camping with the Scouts on Flat Holm this summer," he said.

"That tiny island in the Bristol Channel?" asked Mark. "Lucky beggar! Could we go, do you think?"

"John says it's only for Scouts. There isn't any fresh-water supply there, or anything. He doesn't think anyone lives there any more. There are wild goats roaming about, though."

"Sounds great," said Mark. "It isn't all that far, is it? I mean, you can easily see it from the beach at Penarth."

"I know," said Simon. "Let's ask Akela to take us there, just for the day. You know he's keen on boats. He's got one with an outboard motor."

"Smashing!" agreed Mark. "Let's ask him tomorrow."

Simon's eyes shone. "I bet he'll say yes." He stopped at his garden gate. "I've promised to help my sister practise her semaphore. She's in the Guides, and she's working for her Signaller Badge. She gets me to see if I understand what she's signalling."

90

"Then you must be learning it too," remarked his friend.

"I hadn't thought of that," said Simon, with a grin. "I suppose I must."

Akela agreed to put the idea of a day on Flat Holm to the Pack at the next meeting. When he asked them what they thought, he put his hands over his ears at the enthusiastic response.

"Ask your parents about it," he said, "and let me know which of you can come."

The following week he asked the Pack: "Now, how many are definitely coming?" He counted the raised hands. "That's nine of us altogether. The boat should just about take that many. Now for the lists." He went through various items of food and drink. Then he turned to Mark. "You've gained your First Aider badge, Mark. Will you make up an emergency first-aid kit— bandages, plaster, safety-pins—you know the sort of thing?"

"Yes, Akela."

"It's like going to a desert island," said Tiny, a small Cub Scout, happily.

"Don't forget your eight records, then," said Jem, in a sneering tone.

Akela looked at Jem's scowling face. "If you want to come, Jem, you must pull your weight and not cause trouble," he said quietly.

Simon and Mark exchanged glances. These said as plainly as words, "If only Jem wasn't coming!" When they were locking up the Scout headquarters later, after the rest had gone, Mark said, "Is Jem really coming, Akela?"

"If he wants to, he can come," Akela said. "It's up to us to make him a better member of our Pack, isn't it?"

The morning of the expedition dawned bright and sunny. The boys assembled at the landing-stage, where Akela was waiting with the boat. Under Akela's watchful eye, the Cubs went aboard. Nobody tripped up or fell in the water! Once aboard, with food

Supervised by Akela, the Cubs boarded the boat

They dropped overboard, holding up their shoes

and equipment settled, Akela started up the motor. Out in the Bristol Channel they could see the flat shape of the island in the morning mist.

"It isn't very big," said Akela as they chugged away from the shore, "just about six hundred yards long and almost as wide. It's a jolly interesting place, though. Anyone good at history?" He looked round at them. "Well, the murderers of Thomas à Becket are said to be buried there."

"There's a lighthouse too, isn't there, Akela?" asked Mark.

"Yes, there used to be lots of wrecks, and once sixty soldiers were drowned when their ship was wrecked. After that they put up a lighthouse—years ago, in 1783."

"My sister said they used to send people there who had cholera," said Simon.

"Yes, there was a cholera hospital there. And there's one more thing for you radio fans to remember. It was from Flat Holm that Marconi transmitted the first wireless message across water to Lavernock."

Mark looked impressed. "What was the message, Akela?"

Akela laughed. "It was short and snappy. It said, 'Are you ready?' It might have been meant for us, mightn't it? That was way back in 1897, and you can see the signed copy in the museum in Cardiff."

Jem, hanging over the side, nearly toppled overboard as the boat dipped sharply.

"Sit up, Jem!" said Akela sharply.

Jem muttered under his breath and trailed his fingers in the water. They were nearing the island now, and Akela said, "Large boats can't get near, as these waters are so shallow. Even we shall have to wade ashore. Careful now! We'll haul the boat in afterwards."

One by one they lowered themselves over the side, holding their shoes high and squealing at the coldness of the water. Once ashore, they clambered up the rocks. They could see a grassy slope, then open moorland with coarse scrub and bracken.

They scattered in all directions, looking for the landmarks Akela had told them about, and enjoying the feeling of freedom. Simon and Mark climbed to the highest point and looked towards the mainland.

"Look at the size of those waves," cried Mark.

"It's getting rough," said Simon. "Look how it's moving the boat about." They both stared at the boat, which Akela had fastened firmly with a rope to a huge boulder.

Akela called them to start collecting

wood to make a fire. "The sausages will take some time to cook," he said, "so we must get the fire going." He glanced up at the sky, where clouds were beginning to gather. The wind too had got up, and had quite an edge to it. "Bother!" he added. "I've left the sausages in the boat. Jem, you're not doing anything special, are you? Fetch the sausages from the boat, will you?"

Rather sulkily, Jem walked to the boat. "The boat ought to be pulled farther in," he said, but no one took any notice. Grumbling, he unfastened the rope and tried to drag the boat farther in to the shore. The boat, however, was too heavy, so he tied it up again and returned to Akela with the sausages.

The other Cubs gathered driftwood and dry sticks, and soon there was a crackle and some red flames. "Wait until you get a good glow," said Akela; "otherwise the sausages will taste smoky."

While the meal was cooking, Simon and Mark collected wild flowers, thrift and sea-campion. Gulls wheeled and swooped over the shore.

"It's a smashing place, isn't it?" said Simon.

Mark nodded.

When they came back, the wind had risen and dark clouds were scudding across the sky. As Akela filled their plates with the crackling sausages, he said, "I don't like the look of the weather, boys. We won't leave it too late before starting back."

The Cubs looked at the freshening waves and agreed reluctantly, though Jem grumbled that they hadn't had a chance to

"I don't like the look of the weather," said Akela as he filled the Cubs' plates with sizzling sausages

explore the island. Then a low rumble of thunder in the distance made up Akela's mind.

"That's it, then, boys. Let's prepare to leave. We don't want to be caught in a thunderstorm."

They were all soon busy clearing up and packing away—with the exception of Jem, who slipped away to explore the island. They carefully stamped out the fire, and then Akela said, "Is everyone here?"

Someone said, "Where's Jem?"

Akela called out, "Jem! Come on! We're going now."

There was no reply—only the rising whine of the wind was heard, and a clap of thunder that made them jump. Akela looked worried.

"Where on earth is he? Simon, you and Mark look up there, and I'll go this way. The rest of you go down to the boat."

Breathless with running and calling, Simon and Mark came back at last to where they could see the boat. Then they cried out.

"The boat!" yelled Simon. "It's adrift!"

"The rope's come loose," cried Mark.

It was true. Akela and the Cubs stared aghast as the boat, loosed from its moorings, floated away from the shore. Before they could do anything about it, a huge wave carried it inshore and dashed it against the rocks. Jem, who had suddenly appeared, ran down and caught the rope, but the damage was done. A gaping hole in the side of the boat was letting the sea pour through. The Cubs hauled it ashore, and Akela examined it.

"It's too bad to use, isn't it, Akela?" asked Simon.

Akela nodded. "Everything seems to have happened at once," said Akela. "At any rate, Jem's back. However did I come to leave that mooring-rope like that?"

"The boat's adrift!" yelled Simon

"I—I'm afraid it was me, Akela," Jem said, looking shamefaced. "I tried to pull the boat farther in, and I must have tied the rope round the boulder too loosely."

"Well, that's an honest admission," said Akela, "and I think all the more of you for owning up, Jem. Now we've got to find a way of getting off the island. We'll have to attract attention somehow."

"Shall we make a fire again?" asked Simon. "A passing ship might see that."

"Good idea," said Akela. "Bring the brushwood down here and we'll make a good blaze—unless the rain puts a stop to it," he added.

The thunder continued to rumble, but the rain kept off. Soon a good fire was blazing. One ship passed by without stopping, although everyone shouted at the top of his voice. The wind carried the sound away.

After a long wait, another ship came into sight, nearer the island. It slowed down and the Cub Scouts waved frantically. Then a man on board tried to hail them through a megaphone, but no sound reached them over the roar of the wind and the thunder. They pointed to their smashed boat, but those on board clearly didn't understand.

Suddenly Mark said, "What about semaphore, Akela? You could signal to them!"

Akela pursed his lips. "I could if I knew how, but I'm sorry to say I've forgotten all my semaphore."

Mark gave a cry. "Simon knows semaphore—don't you, Simon?"

Simon nodded eagerly. "I'll need two sticks and two good big hankies."

Everyone turned out pockets, and soon Simon was tying a handkerchief on the end of each long stick. The men on board the ship had put down their megaphone and were gazing at the island.

Simon took up his stand on the most prominent point he could find, then raised his arms and began to signal.

SOS, he spelt out. BOAT WRECKED. HELP.

At once the watching Cubs could see activity taking place on board the ship. Then one of the crew waved flags in reply.

"What's he saying?" asked Mark.

"Half a minute!" said Simon, his eyes fixed on the flags. "HELP COMING!" he translated triumphantly.

"Well done, Simon!" said Akela. "Jolly well done!"

A huge wave lifted the boat and dashed it against the rocks

The Cubs cheered as Akela patted Simon's back.

"I say, Jem," murmured Mark, "I'm rather glad we've got to be rescued. It's quite an adventure."

Jem looked glum, then began to grin. "I see what you mean," he said.

The watching boys saw a small boat leave the ship and make rapidly for the island. Soon it crunched on the shingle. The young officer in charge grinned as the Cubs ran towards him.

"Nice bit of signalling," he said. "Who did it?"

Akela pushed Simon forward.

"Good lad!" said the officer, smiling. "Had a bit of trouble, have you?" he asked, casting a keen eye over the damaged boat.

Akela explained about the mishap.

"We'll soon have you all ashore," said the officer cheerfully, "and we'll take your boat in tow." A loud clap of thunder came, and he added, with a smile, "Getting cross up there, isn't he? Now in you all get!"

It was rather a squash, but they all managed to fit into the boat, which was soon speeding towards the mainland with the damaged boat in tow.

When they landed, Akela thanked the officer and crew heartily, and the Cubs waved as the boat sped back to the ship.

The rain that had threatened for so long began to pour down in earnest.

"We'll all go straight home," said Akela. "We'll see about repairs to the boat later. We've had an exciting day, anyhow."

"I'll say we have," agreed Simon, as he set off homeward with Mark. "What say you, Jem?" he asked, as they joined the lone figure of Jem, who had already started off. "Have you enjoyed yourself?"

Jem nodded. "I say, Simon, how about teaching me semaphore?" he asked, rather hesitantly. "I'd love to be able to send messages, like you did today."

"Sure I'll help you learn it," said Simon, readily. "So will my sister. She'd be jolly glad to have someone else to practise with. We'll talk about it at next Pack meeting, eh?"

"Thanks," said Jem. "I'll look forward to that."

When he turned off for his own home, Mark looked after him and whistled. "I reckon our day out has done something for Jem," he remarked. "Your signalling's got him interested, Simon."

Simon nodded. "I've got an idea that we shan't have any more trouble with Jem," he said.

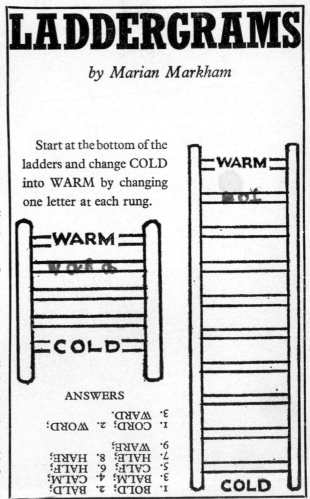

LADDERGRAMS

by Marian Markham

Start at the bottom of the ladders and change COLD into WARM by changing one letter at each rung.

WARM

COLD

WARM

COLD

ANSWERS

1. CORD; 2. WORD; 3. WARD.

1. BOLD; 2. BALD; 3. BALM; 4. CALM; 5. CALF; 6. HALF; 7. HALE; 8. HARE; 9. WARE.

CUB SCOUT GAMES

by EILEEN CHIVERS

NEW YEAR RESOLUTIONS

Equipment needed: 1 set of cards bearing names of people—e.g., a mother, a baby, a policeman, a schoolboy, a pop star, etc.; 1 set of cards bearing corresponding New Year resolutions.

Cub Scouts stand in a circle, one set of cards at one side, the other set at the opposite side. All skip round and sing, to the tune of "I Saw Three Ships":

I made a resolution
On New Year's Day, on New Year's Day,
I made a resolution
On New Year's Day in the morning.

They stop, and the one nearest to each set of cards picks up the top one and reads it out. Amusing results will occur, such as:
Policeman: I resolve to go to bed without my dummy.
Baby: I resolve to give up smoking.

PANCAKE RACE

Equipment needed for each Six: 1 small frying-pan, 1 circle of cardboard slightly smaller than the pan, 1 chair.

Sixes line up in files at one end of the room. A chair is placed in front of each Six, about twelve feet away, a pan and a "pancake" on each chair.

Cub Scouts run up in turn, toss the pancake, catch it, and return to their place.

The first team to finish wins.

OCTOBER LEAVES

When the Cub Scouts arrive for their weekly meeting they find that lots of leaves are blowing about on the path in front of the Scout headquarters. They do a good turn by sweeping them up, and later on they play the following game.

Equipment needed: Large leaves cut from brown paper or cardboard. On the backs of two of them the word BROOM is written.

Cubs stand in a ring. Each one is given a leaf. They turn them over to see if they are BROOMS, but they must not tell. All skip round and sing to the tune of "London Bridge is falling down":
October leaves are falling down, falling down,
  falling down,
October leaves are falling down,
My fair lady!

All LEAVES run to one end of the room, and the BROOMS catch as many as they can. The ones caught lose a "life", and the game continues with different BROOMS.

THE BOGUS JOBBERS

A SCOUT JOB WEEK ADVENTURE IN PICTURES

YOU'VE BEEN PRETENDING TO BE CUB SCOUTS AND TAKING MONEY FOR JOBS
AND YOU'VE KEPT MONEY GIVEN TO YOU FOR SHOPPING!
WE'D BETTER SCRAM, BERT. COME ON!
'ERE, CUB SCOUT, YOU CAN 'AVE MY ICECREAM!
LOOSE ME OR I'LL KNOCK YOU SILLY!
NOT SO FAST, LONGLEGS!
HELP, CONSTABLE! THESE LADS ARE FIGHTING!
DOWN YOU GO, SHORTY!
WOW!

THINGS TO MAKE FOR BRONZE ARROW

(Simple Handicrafts)

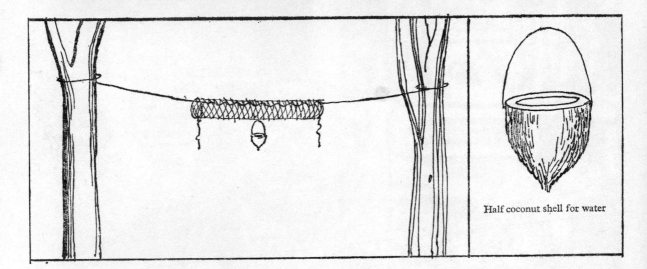

Half coconut shell for water

A BIRD HAMMOCK
by M. I. Eckhardt

Our feathered friends the wild birds need your love and care all the year round. In winter-time they need bread, scraps and water (not ice). In summer-time they also need bread, scraps and water. This is particularly necessary during dry spells.

To help the birds get their food easily and safely it is a good idea to make a bird hammock. You will need a piece of rope or thick string, a piece of wire-netting 18" wide × 12" long and a piece of thin wire.

Fasten the rope between two long nails driven into a wall—or between two trees in the garden. Fasten the wire-netting around the rope as shown in the drawing and then secure with thin wire. To place food inside, you can either push it in from the ends, or untie the wire and then refasten it. Don't forget to include in your scraps, when you can, chicken carcases, bacon rind cut up, bones from weekend joint with scraps of meat on, peanuts (hung on strings at intervals), sunflower seedheads (dried).

Make sure the hammock is hung well away from the reach of any cats. It is also a good idea to hang it where you can get a good view of it yourself. After all, it would be a pity to miss any rare birds you tempt into the garden.

A PENCIL CASE
by Muriel Wallington

You will need 2 empty washing-up-liquid bottles (the same), large needle, modelling knife, warm water. Remove the writing from the plastic bottles with

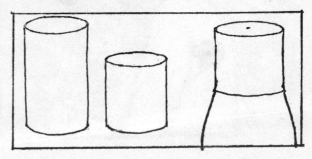

scouring powder. Make a mark round one bottle $5\frac{1}{2}$ inches from the bottom, and make a mark on the other one 3 inches from the bottom. Cut round bottles on these marks and throw the tops away.

With the needle make a hole in the centre of the smaller piece. Now dip the cut edge of the smaller piece in fairly warm water for a short while and then push the plastic down over a glass bottle to stretch it slightly. A milk bottle or a large squash bottle may be large enough.

You will find when it has been stretched it will fit on to the piece $5\frac{1}{2}$ inches tall to make a case for your pencils. It can be left plain or be decorated with paints.

A USEFUL FILE
by W. I. Smith

A simple file for putting your photographs and the like in order is easily made out of an exercise-book—old or new.

Cut each alternate page down a little. Now join the shorter page to the longer page behind it, at the edges, with a piece of sticky tape.

It will not take long to do this, and you will have a very handy reference pocket file when you have finished.

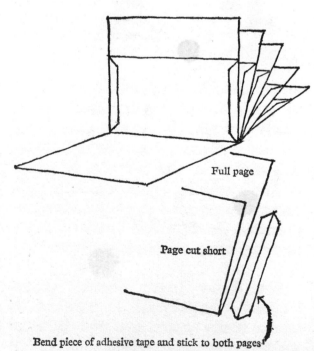

Full page

Page cut short

Bend piece of adhesive tape and stick to both pages

AN INDOOR GARDEN

by M. I. Eckhardt

This indoor garden could be acceptable for the Simple Handicrafts part of Bronze Arrow. To make it you need an egg-carton to hold half a dozen eggs, mustard-and-cress seeds, cotton-wool, paints, scissors and water.

Carefully cut off the lid of the egg-carton. Paint the carton in bright colours. Paint M for mustard and C for cress as a pattern on top when dry. Half fill each section with cotton-wool, then wet with water.

Open your packets of seeds and sprinkle some of the cress seeds into three of the sections. If you want both types of seed to grow at the same time it is better to sow the mustard seeds four days later. Water the cotton-wool whenever it is dry, but not too much or it may soak into your carton and spoil it.

The seeds will soon grow. When they have grown to about $1\frac{1}{2}''$ high, snip them off with the scissors.

Now you can take your mustard-and-cress garden to Pack meeting, show Akela, and then make a tasty sandwich of mustard-and-cress.

Which is your favourite tree? Is it the sturdy oak? Is it the graceful birch, the stately cedar, the beautiful weeping willow?

Here's a charming poem about the weeping willow by Aileen E. Passmore:

> *I've never seen the willow weep,*
> *But I know it does, for, oh!*
> *There's a pool of quiet water*
> *Shining silver down below—*
> *A pool filled with the cool sweet tears*
> *The willow's wept throughout the years.*

I think my own favourite tree is the poplar. As I look out of my window I can see a row of poplars. Each one is stately and graceful, gently aloof from the world of men, from earthly things, as it aspires to the heavens. It seems to be wholly self-sufficient, its branches upturned in prayer; it seems to spend its days and years in quiet contemplation of clouds and stars and sky.

You know Joyce Kimer's poem "Trees", don't you? It was set to music many years ago and became widely known as a result.

WHICH IS YOUR FAVOURITE TREE?

asks
the Editor

Can you identify the trees on these two pages?

TREES

I think that I shall never see
A poem lovely as a tree;

A tree whose hungry mouth is prest
Against the earth's sweet-flowing breast;

A tree that looks at God all day,
And lifts her leafy arms to pray;

A tree that may in summer wear
A nest of robins in her hair;

Upon whose bosom snow has lain;
Who intimately lives with rain.

Poems are made by fools like me,
But only God can make a tree.

Recently, men cut down about ten elm-trees bordering the meadow near my house. It was a sad sight. How long it took for those tall trees to grow, and how quickly their end came! Now the rooks must seek another home, and I must avert my eyes from the gap that the fallen elms have left.

Thank goodness, we have many grand and beautiful trees and woods left. Let's cherish them, remembering that they can be cut down in a day or an hour but take a human lifetime to grow to full glory.

—**R.M.**

SPLASHDOWN FOR THE BLACK SIX

by RIKKI TAYLOR

The Black Sixer walked near the front

"Splashdown will be at 17.00 hours," announced Akela. "Then, by kindness of the astronauts, you Cubs can attempt to link the module with the spacecraft."

Ian Towse, the Black Sixer, gave a mischievous grin. "Is splashdown in the Pacific, Akela?"

His eyes twinkling, the Cub Scout Leader answered: "No. This time we expect it in the River Nive."

A cheer rose from the circle of Cubs, who guessed that this latest project was going to be fun. Their Leaders often arranged outdoor activities based on interesting events, but this was the first time they had ventured into "space". Not only were they about to set out on a hike, which would include a bathe in the River Nive, but the Leaders had planned even more fun for the afternoon.

"What d'you think this spacecraft link-up thing will be?" asked Simon, the Black Second, as he and the Sixer marched along near the front of the excited Cubs.

"Dunno!" replied Ian. "But I can make a guess about the astronauts. Bagheera and Kim are missing!"

Simon threw a quick glance at the three Leaders, walking at spaced intervals along the line of Cubs: Akela at the front, Baloo near the middle, and Rikki bringing up the rear. Bagheera and Kim were not with the Pack. Those two bright and gay Venture Scouts never missed an outing; they must be absent for a special reason.

"You're right," agreed Simon. "Bagheera and Kim could be planning a drop from outer space into the River Nive. They'll be doing the splashdown."

After the long, hot, dusty hike, the Cubs enjoyed their own splash in the cool, sparkling water of the river, and the wooded valley rang with their shouts. As they patrolled the banks, Rikki paused a moment to whisper to Akela.

"Where are our two astronauts? I can't see anything of them."

"Oh, they'll be keeping well hidden," replied the Cub Scout Leader. "Bagheera and Kim planned to jump from the highest branches of that big oak overhanging the river—just there, by the bend. Beneath the tree is a nice, deep pool into which they can jump safely. They won't want to stay in hiding up the tree all the afternoon; they'll probably climb it while the Cubs are having tea in the hollow along the bank here."

When the time came to eat their packed tea, the Cubs were far too hungry to notice anything that might be happening farther along the riverside. After the hike and the swim they all had good appetites. As the last crumbs disappeared, Akela, looking at his watch, called out: "It's just five minutes to splashdown. Collect all your paper, pack your rucsacs, and follow me. We should get a good view from this bank."

Eager to enter into the fun of the mock splashdown, the Pack hastened to obey Akela's orders. By 16.58 hours they had cleared every scrap of litter from the

The Cubs lined up by the river for the countdown

picnic site, and were lined along the riverside, close to the old oak.

"Sixteen-fifty-nine hours," Akela called out. "Ready for the countdown?"

In unison, the Cubs chanted: "Ten-nine-eight-seven-six-five-four-three-two-one-ZERO!"

At their last loud shout, startled birds fluttered from the trees. But nothing else happened! There was no space-ship, no splashdown, no astronauts.

"What's gone wrong?" muttered Baloo.

"Perhaps their timing has gone haywire," suggested Akela in a loud voice. "Come on, boys; we'll try again."

If anything, the repeat of "ZERO" was even louder this time; it sent a ripple through the leaves of the old oak, but it did nothing else.

"Oh, dear!" murmured Akela. "Something somewhere has gone wrong with the plans."

"Have they got the wrong stretch of river?" asked Rikki. "Coming from outer space, it must all look pretty much alike."

Akela shrugged, then called out: "Right,

Pack! Until we can make contact with the astronauts you can go for a scramble in the woods. Points will be given to the Six which brings back the longest piece of grass."

"Blacks! Blacks! Come on, Blacks!" called their Sixer. He led his Six into the woods to a wide ditch that ran parallel with the river. Although the ditch was now dry, the spring moisture had given it a good growth of grass and other vegetation.

Pointing to it, Ian said quietly: "We should find some long pieces in this ditch. Don't let the others see us—we don't want all the Pack to follow."

The Blacks slipped stealthily down, and only the wavering of the long grass marked their progress along the ditch. They had only gone a few yards when Ian, who was leading, thrust out his arms to hold back the rest of the Six.

"Hi! What's this?" he hissed. Then, grinning, he added: "I think I've seen these Scout shirts before."

The Blacks clustered round, staring down at the two heaps of clothing lying in a dry part of the ditch. Simon, the Second, picked up one of the shirts. Fingering the badges on the sleeve, he chuckled.

"Kim's, for sure! Look at this County Badge! He played havoc with me last Pack night when I almost tore it off in Stonehenge Rugby. Wait till I see Kim—he hasn't sewn it back on yet!"

Ian had been staring thoughtfully down at the piles of clothing. Now he too chuckled.

"They will have changed into their wet suits. They'll look just like astronauts."

"What are wet suits?" asked Freddie, a newcomer to the Pack.

"What people wear for water sports," explained Ian. "They're made in one piece, they're very tight-fitting and they're waterproof. When sailing or canoeing or anything like that they're a lot warmer than just a swimsuit."

"Kim and Bagheera use theirs for water-ski-ing and skin-diving," put in Simon. "Their suits are black, and they have helmets and goggles. They look just like spacemen."

While his Second was describing the Venture Scouts' wet suits, Ian made a close examination of the ground farther along the ditch. As the Blacks scrambled towards him, the Sixer again flung out his arms to hold them back.

"Funny!" He frowned. "The trail goes in the opposite direction from what I expected."

The path of flattened grass along the bottom of the ditch was clear enough for anyone to see. It had obviously been made by the trampling feet of Kim and Bagheera. But why did it lead further down-river,

Ian cast a quick look down

away from the area where the splashdown had been arranged?

With the Blacks strung in a line behind, Ian crept along the trail. Then Freddie's leg caught in a bramble. He let out a yelp of pain. The Sixer spun round and put a warning finger to his lips.

"Hush, hush!" he whispered. "Remember what Baloo told us about tracking? A good Scout moves silently when he's on a trail."

Nods of agreement came from all the Blacks, and they moved forward with only the noise of one or two breaking twigs. Intent on watching their steps, they scarcely realised that the ditch was faithfully following a curve in the river and that they were drawing close to the bank just above a weir. At each side of this weir were square concrete boxes through which streams of water trickled; these had been built to help the salmon in their leap up the weir as they journeyed upstream. The Nive was noted for its fine salmon fishing, and a licence to fish it could cost as much as five hundred pounds.

As they drew level with the weir, Ian slipped noiselessly out of the ditch and cast a quick look at the deep pool that lay below. There, the tumbling waters became quiet and still. His face broke into a wide grin as he saw two black-clad figures by the side of the weir. He slid back into the ditch, again put a finger to his mouth, and whispered: "Kim and Bagheera are just down there, by the riverside. You know how they always say we're no good at stalking? Well, we'll surprise 'em. Let's see how close we can get before they hear us."

The Blacks grinned their agreement. It was not often they got a chance to try and better the two Venture Scouts. Flat on their fronts, slowly, inch by inch, the six Cubs edged their way to the top of the ditch. Hardly daring to breathe, they

There were two black-clad figures by the side of the weir

A hand clamped across his mouth

glided through the thick grass. Ian, who was leading, raised his head to chance a quick peep into the water below. Good! The two figures were still by the edge of the pool—but what were they carrying in their hands? Those long things looked like spears!

"Spears?" muttered Ian. "Spears?"

The Black Sixer dropped flat, and crept on once more. He was about to slide over the edge when suddenly a hand shot out from a clump of bushes. It grabbed one of Ian's ankles while another hand clamped across his mouth and strong arms pulled him into the bushes.

"Not a sound!" came an urgent whisper.

Ian could not stifle his gasp of surprise—and relief. His captors were Kim and Bagheera.

"You? You here? You should be down there—by the water."

Kim and Bagheera realised what he meant, but they were too busy to answer; they were intent on gathering the rest of the Blacks—in silence—into the cover of the bushes. Fortunately, the few sounds they made were drowned by the noise of the gurgling water rushing over the weir.

Only when all eight of them were crouched together in the bushes did Bagheera attempt an explanation.

"We were getting changed in the ditch," he told them, "when those two slid by us. We followed them. We think they must be poachers. Poaching salmon is big business in a river like the Nive. I think they're hunting the salmon and spearing them underwater."

With his mouth close to Simon's ear, Kim whispered:

"Take Freddie and one of the other Cubs. Get back to Akela—as fast as you can go. Tell him what's happening here. The other three can stay with us—we may need them."

Bagheera and Kim did need them. As the two poachers stood, poised, ready to dive and strike their quarry, the Venture Scouts leapt out of the bush and jumped down the river-bank. With a flying tackle, each made a grab for the legs of one of the poachers. In a flash the four black-clad figures were a whirling mass of arms and legs. There were heavy thumps, grunts and groans. Ian and the two remaining Blacks danced above, shouting with excitement. They could not see whether the two Venture Scouts were bettering their opponents; in their black wet suits all four looked alike.

But there was no mistaking Kim's triumphant grin as he sat astride the helpless form of one of the poachers, or Bagheera's shout from the back of the other prone figure.

"Hi, Cubs! Down here—quick. Pass us your neckers."

With a few expert twists of the neckerchieves the Venture Scouts tied the hands of the poachers behind their backs.

"Is this any use?" asked Ian, holding out a length of cord.

Bagheera grinned, and used it to tie the feet of one of the poachers.

"Glad to see you observe the Scout motto—Be Prepared!"

The other two Blacks found cord in their pockets, so the Venture Scouts soon made a firm job of tying up the two captives. Keeping a wary eye on the prisoners, Bagheera said: "The water-bailiff will be glad we've solved a problem for him. It's been worrying him. He guessed the salmon-poachers were using a new method. They usually operate only at night, and he hadn't thought of looking for them in the daytime."

The water-bailiff was delighted at the capture of the poachers, and the police, summoned by Akela, were quite happy to find the job done for them.

"Splashdown in the Nive!"

There was a rush to assemble as Akela

The four black-clad figures were soon a whirling mass of arms and legs

Two figures fell into the deep water

called "Pack! Pack! Pack!" from the oak-tree.

Next came the suspense of the count-down, ending with the shout of "ZERO!"

This time there was a response.

As if from the skies, something shaped like a spaceship dropped down and splashed into the river, where it was carried gently along by the stream.

Seconds later came two human figures, who fell from above into the depths of the pool.

"Hurrah!" shouted the Cubs. "Hurrah for the astronauts!"

With strong crawl-strokes the two black-clad figures raced after the space-craft, secured it with a rope, and towed it to the river-bank. Then they climbed out of the water, the thick vizors of their helmets hiding their faces.

"Are they really astronauts?" asked one of the younger Cubs, in awe.

"No! They're Kim and Bagheera," Simon told him.

All the Cubs were surprised when the two black-suited figures began roping to-gether the two silvered milk-churns, which had looked so like a spacecraft. The base had been removed from one of the churns, and the top of the other hung close to it, about five feet above ground-level.

Speaking in a muffled voice, Bagheera explained to the Pack, "As you can see, one of these craft is the mother ship; the other is a module. We shall hoist a Cub astride each. By gently swinging, they will try to link up the two craft."

The Cubs clamoured loudly to be al-lowed to go first. Both astronauts shook their heads.

"Blacks will try first," stated Bagheera. "This is their reward for observing a trail, following it skilfully, and helping two astronauts to capture poachers and save the salmon."

Generously, as Ian and Simon led the Blacks towards the water, the Pack cheered.

THIS AND THAT

Why is the bride always sad on her wedding-day? *Because she doesn't marry the best man.*

AKELA (inspecting Pack): You haven't washed your face, Billy. I can see what you had for breakfast.
BILLY: What did I have, Akela?
AKELA: Egg.
BILLY: Wrong. That was yesterday.

JOHNNY: What's the name of the place where they're building an eye hospital?
TONY: A site for sore eyes.

THE EDITOR'S CHAT

One of the "ghost" railways   Photo: Robert Moss

I live in a country lane, and you'd be astonished at the number of interesting happenings I see and hear about, although some people think the country is dull!

The cows in the meadow next to my house are most amusing. I fill their trough with water from an outside tap in my garden, and they are glad to drink the water; but they constantly try to nose out the hose that brings the water to the trough. They don't like it there, and they push at it until they manage to get it out. Well, it's got to be in the trough, or there won't be any water there for them. What I have done is to fasten string round the end of the hose and attach the other end to a heavy brick, which lies in the bottom of the trough and is too heavy for the cows to lift out! That, so far, has done the trick; the cows nose at the hose in vain; the brick holds it down!

A new pony, a high-spirited dapple-grey, has recently arrived in the meadow. He is young and rather frisky. He likes apples and sugar, but steps towards me very gingerly when I bring some out for him to eat. He won't have anything to do with cows. Oh, dear, no! He thinks he's much superior to cows. He grazes on his own away from them. If they come near him he chases them away. As he is such a spirited pony, I was very surprised one day to see him being ridden safely and steadily by his owner, who is only six years old!

When I took some Cub Scouts and Brownies to a donkey farm last year, I bought carrots for the donkeys. Just as we were about to leave, I thought I saw one of the Brownies' berets in the field, so I ran to get it. Some yards before I reached it, I realised that it wasn't a beret at all, but a tuft of grass or something like that. So I stopped, and as I did so something biffed me hard in the back. I pitched forward, and then looked round. Do you know what had bumped me in the back? A donkey! Without my knowing it, when I began to run for the beret, Mr Hee-Haw set off after me, doubtless hoping for a few more carrots. When I stopped suddenly he didn't, and so gave me a foul blow in the back!

During the past few years many branch-line railways have been closed and have fallen into disuse. I love

Brock the badger   Photo: T. Holloway

exploring these forgotten railway tracks. You can often walk for miles and miles along them. How about suggesting to Akela that the Pack explore the "ghost" railways? They are free from traffic of any kind, and some of them lead through lovely country and are full of wild flowers, grasses and pretty vegetation of all kinds. They are the home of wild creatures too. I was walking one afternoon along the disused railway track between the Cotswold villages of Withington and Chedworth when out from the bushes trotted a full-grown fox. He took no notice of me, but padded on into the bushes on the other side of the track and then into a meadow. I watched him as he ran up the side of the meadow and then across a ridge at the top and into a wood. It was quite a thrill to me to see a fox in broad daylight at close quarters like that.

I nearly saw another fox one afternoon when I was strolling through Miserden Park, in Gloucestershire. It sounds silly, doesn't it, to say "I nearly saw a fox", because you either see one or you don't. What I did see was a large reddy-brown animal, which crossed the roadway on which I was walking. For a moment I thought it was a fox, but when I came to think about it I felt sure it was a hare I had seen. It leapt across my path so quickly and vanished so completely in the undergrowth on the other side that I had only a fleeting glimpse of it, but I realised afterwards that its movements, as well as its size, were those of a hare.

One day a van stopped in a lane where I happened to be, and two men got out. They told me that one of their jobs was to clean out the culverts at the sides of the lane, to ensure that the water ran away freely and didn't overflow into the lane. They told me that they quite often found badgers in the culverts. These delightful, harmless animals with striped heads find the culverts a useful ready-made home and so decide to move in—until the cleaners come along and move them out! The cleaners don't hurt them; one of the men assured me that he loved animals and wouldn't harm them for the world. The badgers just pad off and look for another vacant house!

Traffic today does cause the death of many animals, especially perhaps the slow-moving hedgehog; but I was very amused one day as I drove along a busy main road to see a squirrel sitting on his haunches on the grass-verge calmly chewing a nut and taking not the slightest notice of the streams of cars and lorries rushing by!

Turning off the main road, I drove down a lane and then into a field through which was a rough track that led to one of those derelict railway-tracks I've been telling you about. Halfway over the field, I became bogged down in mud and couldn't get out. I stepped out of the car to see what I could do to extract the wheels from the mud, and saw a policeman running across the field towards me. For a moment I thought he was going to arrest me. He'd seen me come across the field and came after me to find out whether I was going to dump a lot of rubbish somewhere. I assured him that I never ever left even as much as a toffee paper in the countryside. I hate to see litter scattered over our lovely land. The policeman was so convinced that I was a lover of the country, and not a litterer of it, that he very kindly stayed and helped me get out of my mud-bath!

Finally, here's a quaint bit of information for those of you who feed birds in your garden. It you want to give them a special treat put out some custard for them in a shallow dish. They simply love custard. I've been sharing my pudding custard with the birds every day for a long time, and they've never yet left a speck in the dish! The sparrows perch in a row on the side of the dish, and even queue up for their turn to have a peck.

Well, I'd better stop "The Editor's Chat" or I'll have to alter the title to "The Editor's a Chatterbox"! —R.M.

Reynard the fox   *Photo: Eric Hosking*

ARE BOTH YOUR EYES OPEN?

Hints on How to Train Your Eyes, Ears and Memory Day by Day

Cub Scouts used to be called Wolf Cubs, and they had to pass tests before they could wear stars on their cap. When they gained one star they were said to have one eye open, and when they won their second star they had both eyes open.

Are both *your* eyes open? Train yourself to observe. Study the people you meet on the bus or in the street— not by staring at them rudely, of course!

Note, if you can, hands, clothes, hats, shoes? Can you tell from these what kind of work he or she does? Are you looking at a tidy or an untidy person, a townsman or a country dweller?

If you observe a friend or a relative you can often find out whether your deductions were correct, but even if you can't do that with strangers you have begun to cultivate the habit of observing.

For the Cub Scout Naturalist badge and the Explorer badge you not only have to learn to observe, but you have to remember too. In working for the Observer badge, Scouts play Kim's Game, in which they have to remember twenty-four out of thirty different objects they have looked at for only one minute. Try this game with your Six and see how hard remembering can be—and how quickly you can improve with practice. B.-P. set this test for Scouts after reading Rudyard Kipling's story of Kim, a poor orphan who began training for the Indian Secret Service in this way.

Even if you are only in a room you can cultivate observation and memory. Give yourself five minutes to memorise every detail of a room. Study everything you can see through the window; look for details in a picture; note the leaf formation of plants in the window.

You can train your hearing further by listening in the dark. Learn to hear noises and identify them, both out of doors and indoors. Ask a friend to join you and practise recognising noises when blindfolded. Jangle keys, scrape a foot, drop a coin, and see who can tell what the sound is. Make noises harder to distinguish by dropping a rubber, clicking your teeth, or turning over the leaves of a book. In time you will be swift to recognise every sound you hear.

Instead of looking blankly ahead on

your way to school or when waiting at a bus stop—or *thinking* blankly!—try observing things and people. How many houses are there with slate roofs, how many with tiles on? Are there any pillar boxes of unusual design or of ancient date? What time does the next post go? Are there any speed-limit or no-parking signs? What's the name of that church? Is the post-office open and does it close in the lunch hour—if so, at what time?

On a car journey, notice A.A. and R.A.C. boxes, signposts and warning notices. On a railway journey observe plate-layers' huts, uncommon locomotives, mailbag and other apparatus along the line or at stations. If you don't know what some of the objects are, remember them and find out about them. This will not only train your faculties; it will make your journey most interesting. At the end, spend a few moments summing up what you have noticed. See if you can write an account of your journey, including descriptions of the people who were in the compartment or the car with you—how they were dressed, what their features were like, and so on. Sherlock Holmes, the famous fictional detective, astounded people by his acute observation, being able to deduce from things nobody else even noticed quite intimate details about a stranger.

You may care to go on and train the senses of taste, touch and smell. Learn to identify unknown things that are popped into your mouth or held under your nose or which you feel when blindfolded. As you become more efficient, handicap yourself by putting gloves on to feel with, and so on.

If you really persist in practising, you will become a most acute observer —if not a real-life Sherlock Holmes, an alert Cub Scout!

Can You Name Tim's Dog?

Tim, Sixer of the Tawnies, is Irish and he has given his dog an Irish name. Can you find out what it is? You'll be able to spell it out by starting at the bottom of the path and stepping from one crazy paving-stone to the next to reach the line nearest the kennel. You must not leap over stones. —J. W. Gosden

GROW YOUR OWN MISTLETOE

Says E. R. Webber

We all love to have a nice bunch of mistletoe to hang up at Christmas time, don't we? Sometimes we see it growing on apple-trees in an old orchard and wonder how it got there.

Mistletoe is what is called a parasite. That is, it depends on another plant for all its food. You know how sticky mistletoe berries are. Well, birds are fond of these berries, and sometimes one gets stuck on the side of its beak. To get rid of it, the bird goes to another tree and rubs its beak up against the bark. Sometimes this berry (which has a seed inside it) gets into a crack in the bark. It likes it there, so it begins to send roots down right inside the tree. In this way it gets food. Then it starts to send out leaves—and soon we have another clump of mistletoe growing on the tree.

The missel-thrush is supposed to do this more often than any other bird, and maybe that is how the mistletoe got its name.

In the shops at Christmas mistletoe is sometimes quite dear, but by imitating the birds you can grow some for yourself. Get a ripe berry about the end of February or in early March. If you like, you can keep berries from the Christmas bunch. Just leave them in a box, where they can stay until they have ripened off.

Rub the berry into a crack in a tree. An apple-tree is a favourite, but almost any kind will do. If you can't find a good crack, make a small one with a knife. Rub the berry well in and cover it over with a piece of netting or something to keep the birds from pecking it out.

Don't be in too much of a hurry to see a big clump

of mistletoe, though! It is very slow-growing and it may be several years before it is large enough to be cut. But once it is really growing it will probably live for a lifetime—that is if you don't cut it off at one go!

Leave enough every Christmas to enable it to sprout again and grow into another clump, won't you?

LOST IN LONDON —

SIX CUB SCOUTS

Can You Find Them in This Picture?

Cub Scouts—oh, Cub Scouts,
Say, where have you been?
We've been up to London
To see our good Queen.

We've been to the Tower,
And Regent's Park Zoo,
To Buckingham Palace
And Headquarters too.

At Madame Tussaud's
Young Bill gave a squeal
When he tickled a policeman
And found he was real!

The Red Six got lost—
Just what they *would* do!
We found them at last;
Can you find them too?

Now we're home once more,
And all of us say,
What a wonderful trip!
What a wonderful day!

MIKE'S FIRST GOOD TURN

An American Cub Scout Story

by SUE ALEXANDER

Mike looked himself over in the mirror

Mike Brent buckled the new webbed belt carefully, making sure that the shiny Cub Scout emblem was centred properly. Looking himself over carefully in the bathroom mirror, he gave a satisfied tug to the yellow neckerchief. His Bobcat pin gleamed in the overhead light.

"Three days and I still have it upside down," he said glumly. The words of Mr. Scott, the Packmaster, echoed in his head. "When you have done your first good turn you may turn your Bobcat pin right side up . . . but not before!"

What kind of a good turn did he have to do? Mike wondered. His mother had said that defending his sister Tracey on the playground yesterday wasn't a good deed—it was something he would do anyway.

"Well, what is a good turn, anyway?" Mike asked.

Smiling, his mother said, "When you aren't looking for a good turn, that's when you'll find one."

"Today I'm sure not looking for one," Mike told himself, "not with Hallowe'en tonight!" Grinning, he pictured himself as he would appear knocking on doors. He would be the most realistic fake tree that anyone ever saw!

"Mike! You'll be late for your Den meeting!"

"I bet I'm the only one with my Bobcat pin still upside down," Mike thought sadly.

Nevertheless he left hurriedly. It just wouldn't do to be late! Besides, he was going to make his trick-and-treat bag at the meeting this afternoon!

That evening, when the street lights went on, the sidewalks began to fill with fairy princesses, supermen, goblins and witches of all sizes. Soon Mike, complete with branches and leaves, joined the

Murphy looked down at him sadly.

"I'm sorry, honey, but there's no more candy," she said. "Some big boys came and took my whole bowl of candy! I never should have put it outside. I guess I'd better turn off my porch light."

Mike felt sorry for Mrs. Murphy. He

"Trick or treat?" asked Mike through a knothole in the crepe-paper tree-trunk

groups going from door to door.

"Trick or treat!" Mike spoke from a knothole in the crepe-paper tree-trunk. His pumpkin-coloured bag, covered with black cats and eerie skeletons, filled up rapidly. "I must have a *ton* of candy!" Mike measured the weight of his bag against that of a goblin standing next to him.

Presently Mike found himself back on his own street, knocking at the door of his across-the-street neighbour, Mrs. Murphy. The door opened slowly. Mrs.

knew that she liked to greet all the children in their costumes.

"Mrs. Murphy, it's me, Mike! I already have a ton of candy. Look!" Holding up his bag, Mike opened it wide. As he did so he thought of a way to help Mrs. Murphy. "Go get your bowl," he said excitedly. "I'll put my candy into it so you'll have some for the other children, and you won't have to turn off your light!"

A little later, as he turned toward home with his empty bag, Mike felt warm in-

His mother was holding his Cub Scout shirt out, with the Bobcat pin the right way up

side. He had stayed around Mrs. Murphy's long enough to watch the next trick-and-treaters come to her door. He had seen the happy look on her face as she held out the full bowl of candy.

"I'm back!" Mike called to his mother as he closed the front door.

"Come into your room!" his mother called back.

Mystified, Mike followed the sound of his mother's voice. Entering his room, he was surprised to see his mother holding his Cub Scout shirt. Smiling, she held it out to him.

"My Bobcat pin! It's *right side up*!" Mike jumped up and down in his excitement.

"Your Packmaster told me how you'd helped Mrs. Murphy," said his mother. "Mrs. Murphy was so delighted that she called to tell him."

Later, tucked in his bed, Mike thought, "Now I know what a good turn is—it's helping someone without thinking about it first!" And taking a last look at his right-side-up Bobcat pin, shining in the moonlight, he fell fast asleep.

WHAT IS IT?

This curious creature uses its "hands" as wings. It likes to flit about in the twilight. Sometimes it seems as if it will dash itself against trees or houses, but it never does. Instead, it swerves aside, almost at the last second; it has a kind of built-in radar system that tells it when an obstacle is near. It sleeps upside-down, suspending itself from the branch of a tree by the hooks at the end of its "thumbs". It lives on insects, which it catches in the air. What is it?

Picture Jigsaw

To find out what this picture is, draw or trace the picture in each frame on the left into the blank frame with the same number on the right.

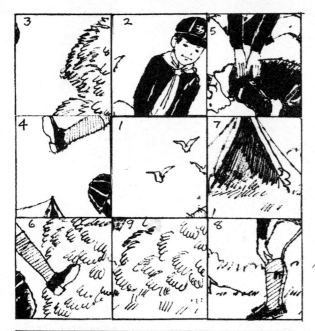

ANSWERS TO PUZZLES

SCOUT
BADGE
PUZZLE
(*page* 26)

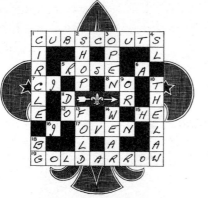

THE SIXER ANNUAL
DOUBLE-PRIZE
COMPETITION

Owing to the large number of entries, it was not possible to publish the result in this annual. The result, however, appeared in the July, 1972, issue of the monthly magazine *Scouting*, published by the Scout Association.

WHAT IS YOUR FAVOURITE TREE? (*pages* 104-5)
1—Weeping Willow, 2—Beech, 3—Birch, 4—Cedar, 5—Oak, 6—Chestnut, 7—Ash, 8—Poplar, 9—Elm

TIME FOR RHYME (*page* 22)

BOOK HOOK	HAT BAT	THRUSH BRUSH	NAIL SAIL	MAP CAP	SWITCH WITCH	BELL SHELL	SADDLE PADDLE
1–11	2–10	3–15	4–12	5–16	6–14	7–13	8–9
BOOK READER	SPORTS-MAN	ARTIST	HANDY-MAN	MAP READER	SCIENTIST	NATURALIST	CYCLIST

NAME THE FLOWERS (*page* 48)
Answers: a, Cowslip; b, Buttercup; c, Kingcup; d, Clover; e, Bluebell

WHAT IS IT? (*page* 124): Bat

RIDDLE-ME-REE (*page* 78)
Camp

FISH CROSSWORD
(*page* 44)

NAME TIM'S DOG
(*page* 118)
Rafferty

125